On

A

Different

Day

L. J. Band

First published in Great Britain in 2016
by L J Band

This edition published on 11ᵗʰ March 2016
by L J Band
Cranbrook Clocks
Unit 2
Northside Yard
Battle Road
Cripps Corner
East Sussex
TN32 5QT

ISBN: 099358490X

A copy of this catalogue is available from the British Library.

Typeset by L J Band

Printed and Bound by L J Band

For

D.E.P. for all the joy you bring me

and

I.S.F. for being supportive always

ON A DIFFERENT DAY

PROLOGUE

In the shadow of the tall bushes, outside the Holmville Estate, on a cold November night, he removed his gloved hand from her mouth, thinking she would be calm, but she emitted a blood-curdling scream. He tightened his gloved grip around her throat to silence the sound but she wouldn't keep still, as he battled against her and the chill, crisp night air that encompassed them. This was his night. This was his moment. He'd meticulously planned it over several months. His adrenaline was pumping. He was anxious, but in control.

She was wriggling and struggling against him. It seemed like only a moment that he had gripped her by the throat, but it was quickly apparent that she was no longer breathing. He panicked. Was she dead? He hadn't meant for her to die. He loosened his grip around her neck and held her head in both his gloved hands. It was apparent that the life was gone from her. He'd wanted to rape her and then let her go but he'd held her neck too tightly. If she hadn't screamed out like that he wouldn't have gripped her neck so tightly. Why did she scream like that?

It was over so quickly. The thrill of the powerful control he had exerted over her in the instant that he seized her was turning to panic as he now looked into her blank, expressionless, eyes. He noticed that her face was luminous white, almost opaque. Her open eyes were staring at him in an accusatory manner. Her mouth fixed open. Forced to look upon her like this, he realised that she was actually quite beautiful. His mood was anxious. He'd just killed her. He hadn't meant to. He didn't know what to do. Right now, his thinking was all over the place. His mind was a fog, while reality, huge, sobering, cold and overwhelming, was looming large. He too was pale now, and in shock. The same thoughts were going round and round in his mind. He'd had no after plan. He'd assumed that after he'd raped her, he'd let her go and he'd go too. He hadn't meant to kill her. He wasn't a killer, but she wouldn't bloody shut up! Bile was rising and filling his throat. He felt like he would choke as the acrid taste of the kebab he'd eaten earlier filled his mouth. He thought he'd be sick. He was gagging and retching. He took a breath.

It seemed like an eternity but could only have lasted a minute or two. He tried to compose himself. He had to regain his composure and reclaim the moment, not snivel like a baby.

Blood rushed to his head. He heard a hissing and ringing in his ears which obscured all other sounds. He saw stars. He felt faint. His heart beat faster and faster, his palms were sweaty beneath the fabric of the gloves. The bitter night air added to the chill that he felt deep inside of him, but it sobered him too, as he became aware of rising floods of panic. "Shit!" He felt himself welling up with tears. "Think, think, think!" He suddenly heard a couple of people walking past. Life was continuing all around him and here he was; stuck in this surreal moment. He looked around sharply, laid the girl's lifeless body quietly in the bushes. Glancing from side to side, he picked up the kitchen knife and slipped it into his pocket, removed the balaclava that he had been wearing and slipped it into his tracksuit pocket, pulled his black fleece hoodie up over his head and ran without a backwards glance. He could see his breath rising in front of him as the November chill encompassed him and he started walking, then jogging towards the canal towpath, as he tried to put distance between himself and the crime that he'd just committed.

This was Camden, north London.

CHAPTER 1

Molly Molson was making cocoa in her kitchen, at the back of her ground-floor flat that overlooked the canal. It was a cold night and she was rationing the heating, as her pension didn't cover the rising cost of living. She was 78 years old and had lived on the Holmville Estate for 35 years. She was a religious woman, of Irish Catholic descent, and she always drank cocoa and said the Rosary before she went to bed. She found it comforting.

Her flat was tiny and smelt musty. The pink wallpaper was peeling in places and added to the general air of shabbiness and decline about the place. It was dusty and dank. The flat was crammed full of her lifetime's mementos; souvenirs of places she'd visited, inexpensive china dogs, cherubs and other figurines, dotted amongst photos of her grandchildren in Ireland. Lacy tablecloths bedecked small tables, her beloved television, which was all she had for company now and a bookcase half-filled with some books were her greatest possessions in life. She called it home. She'd lived here with her husband, Thomas, who had passed away 8 years ago. He'd been a grand fella, had Thomas. Nowadays she lived on her own in perpetual fear of the youngsters that lived on the estate and terrorised the residents. Yet as soon as she chained and bolted her front door she felt relatively safe.

There had been a terrible mugging on the third floor only last year. Her old friend, Betty Quagley had been beaten black and blue. She'd died a month later in hospital and the culprits had never been brought to justice. Then there had been that problem family, where the husband had been found abusing his baby. Truly awful. It made her shudder and she put these thoughts out of her mind.

"If the good Lord wants to take me, he'll take me and I'll be safe in the arms of Jesus forever," she reasoned.

The estate had changed so much over the years though. The community spirit of the old days had gone as people had moved out or passed away and the council placed so-called "problem families" into the flats. The pesky youngsters that bothered everyone rode their bikes into the early hours, shouted abuse, drank alcohol and sprayed graffiti. She knew that some of them carried knives. It was an intimidating atmosphere for older residents brought up in more respectful times. Young hooligans, running wild with no respect for authority and without parental influence. A world away from the London of her youth.

Mrs Molson carried the cocoa into her bedroom, which was at the front of her flat. She placed it on her bedside table and sat down on her bed. It was about 10.00 pm. She had just finished watching her favourite tv comedy and was feeling cheerful. Mrs Molson was turning down the bed covers, about to take her slippers off when she heard a commotion from outside.

A muffled sound, a prolonged struggle, a woman's piercing scream. Then ... nothing. Then running.

Mrs Molson switched off her bedside light and lay back on her bed against the darkness. A shadowy figure ran past her curtains at speed. Her lavatory adjoined the bedroom and she heard a small splash from the other side of the window, as though something had been thrown into the canal.. "Was it a gun, or a knife, or both?" she wondered in fear. She didn't know what to think.

She lay breathing deeply in silent fear, praying that the moment would pass. She didn't know how long she lay there for. It seemed like an eternity. She crossed herself and mumbled, "Oh sweet Jesus keep me safe, oh Holy Mother of God". She was mumbling in short, sharp breaths. After a while she began to calm down. She realised that no harm was going to come to her but she felt fearful and perplexed. What could have happened outside? It must've been something dreadful. Her heart was beating fast. Her hands were trembling. Her eyes fixed upon the crucifix above her bed.

She should call the police, but what if it was one of the local lads who had done this apparent terrible thing and they were to find out that it had been her who had called the police? There could be repercussions: a brick through her window, graffiti outside her flat, faeces pushed through her letterbox ... or worse. Perhaps it was the thugs who'd beaten up Betty Quagley. They were still on the loose. Yet, she felt it was her civic duty to call the police. Her hand reached out towards the telephone. Her hand was shaking. She couldn't hold it out straight and it had nothing to do with the creeping onset of arthritis. "I'll have a sip of cocoa" she thought "it may steady my nerves" and took a sip of the now, stone-cold drink. She found it comforting. In her new-found state of surreal calmness she became aware of a crowd gathering outside and could hear muffled voices. Suddenly sirens pierced the cold night air and flashing blue lights rebounded off her bedroom walls. Vehicle doors opened and slammed shut, and the thud of boots striding quickly along the path could be heard. "Oh thank goodness, someone else must've called the police," she reasoned but she was now in a state of high alertness and curiosity. Sleep couldn't have been furthest from her mind. She went to the window and found the courage to peel back her curtains and peer out upon the scene unfolding before her.

CHAPTER 2

Dr Anthony McCreigh was sitting at his desk in his study, on the first floor of his house. He lived in a large, comfortable, tastefully-furnished Georgian house in Richmond, south-west London, near the River Thames. His silver Mercedes S-Class was parked in the gravel driveway of his house. He was a general practitioner and had his own medical practice in Richmond where his patients mainly consisted of the wealthy, middle-classes, much like himself. He specialised in women's issues, gynaecology and the like.

Dr McCreigh was 5"8 and of a large build. He was 52 years old. His face was wrinkled but handsome. He had thick, grey hair and when he smiled it had been noted that his sparkling blue eyes lit up the room. His family thought he was born to be a doctor. Dr McCreigh was happily married to Vanessa, a minor artist of some renown, who sometimes exhibited her sculptures in trendy art rooms in Chelsea. They had twin daughters, Sophie and Amy, both at different universities. He had lived a good life. Being a wealthy professional who drove a top-of-the-range car, dressed well and enjoyed the finer things in life, women were drawn to him. He was aware of his attractiveness to women and tried to play it down, especially around Vanessa and the girls.

On the whole he had been faithful to Vanessa throughout their 26 year marriage. However he had strayed. He had once had a very low-key affair with his secretary when the children were small. It lasted for a year and was never destined to be anything more than an affair. It ended when this particular secretary met a man who could offer her a more serious future. Dr McCreigh was never going to leave Vanessa. It wasn't the done thing. The affair was merely a distraction while work was particularly stressful and the children were small. He felt guilty for cheating on Vanessa and relieved when the affair was over. He had resolved never to cheat on her again, but then there was the time when he had a different kind of affair. This one was ongoing.

He had met a beautiful woman in a wine bar one night after work. Thumping music resonated in the background as he sat at the bar drinking a whisky and soda.

It had been a particularly stressful day. A charming patient whom he had known for over 15 years had succumbed to cervical cancer. He felt for the family. Then there was another patient to whom he had to give the bad news that test results showed that they had motor neurone disease and probably wouldn't survive beyond the year. Sometimes he hated his job, especially on days like this when bad medical news compounded and lives were torn apart without rhyme or reason. It was for this reason that he was a confirmed atheist. The idea of a merciful God simply didn't exist as far as he was concerned.

The rain was pouring down outside, thick sheets of rain in a mesmerising pattern against the window, as the monotonous London traffic went past. The pounding beat of the music mixed with the alcohol made him feel a little light-headed. He soon became aware of a woman's gaze fixed upon him.

Silvia was South American with silky, long, jet black hair and her size 8 figure was perfectly emphasised by the tight, shiny designer dress that she was wearing. Her make-up was perfectly applied and her long, painted nails gave her an air of elegance. She looked very classy indeed as she walked purposefully towards him and sat next to him. He felt a lump in his throat as he realised how attracted to her he felt. Her almond eyes melted into his and the smell of her perfume intoxicated him. Enveloped in her loveliness, he ordered a round of drinks. His inhibitions were draining from him. He felt emboldened and relaxed and able to forget about the stresses of his day. They spent a couple of hours talking, and he bought more drinks and felt quite content. Silvia spoke almost perfect English, but with a Spanish accent. She told him that she was working as a sales assistant in a department store in Oxford Street. She had lots of funny anecdotes and he found her charming company. She coughed a lot throughout the evening and claimed she had a sore throat. "I'm a doctor, I could check that out for you" he offered.

As soon as he mentioned that he was a doctor Silvia's attitude towards him changed slightly and she seemed nervous. Yet she looked at him with an intense desire in her eyes and he had never felt such intensity before. He knew that she wanted him and he knew that he wanted her so, when he offered to accompany her home in a minicab and she gladly accepted, his heart started beating faster.

The minicab pulled up outside a block of flats in a residential street in Ealing, west London. Silvia shared an apartment here with a room-mate. Thankfully the room-mate was out and no sooner were they through the front door than they began kissing passionately. They fell upon the sofa, gasping and breathing heavily. Things were getting very intense between them and Dr McCreigh's hands were roaming all over Silvia's body. Before his hands could roam more intimately Silvia stopped him suddenly and pulled away. "Look," she said, "I have to be honest with you because I like you a lot." He sat upright and tucked his shirt in. "What is it?" he asked, intrigued.

"I'm ... well ... it's difficult to say and very embarrassing, you being a doctor, you know. I'm sorry. I can't do this. You probably will hate me. You see, I'm, er, I'm a pre-op transsexual," Silvia replied, gazing solemnly at the floor. "Oh," said Dr McCreigh sweeping his hands through his hair, "and are you on hormone therapy treatment?" he felt foolish as he asked, but sometimes he just slipped into the role of doctor so seamlessly.

Silvia nodded. "I am due to have the gender reassignment surgery in two month's time" she replied before continuing "I know it sound like you hear them say a lot, but I do really feel like I'm a woman inside the wrong body," Silvia explained.

Dr McCreigh nodded, sympathetically.

"At the moment my penis is very small, it is shrink," Silvia continued in her slightly pigeon English.

"I see," replied Dr McCreigh.

He now understood that her coughing was to mask her deep voice, which he realised was slightly manly. He could see tears welling up in Silvia's eyes. He sighed. "Come here," he said and wrapped his arms around her. Her vulnerability and sadness at having had to live a life in the wrong gender moved him to tenderness. He turned her face towards him and kissed her gently at first but then more passionately. He could feel desire welling up inside of him again.

"Anthony, you must be crazy!" he thought to himself. "Don't do this!" he reasoned with himself, "You're a happily married man – a professional person. You have no reason to do this. You must stop." But – no, his desire was leading him on. He couldn't help himself, he was simply too excited. The anticipation that he felt about something new and so very different was inexplicable. He wanted to go ahead with this. He unzipped his trousers. "Do you have any lube? Any lubricant?" he elaborated. Silvia rummaged around for a second in her bedside drawer.

"Ok," he said taking it from her and unscrewing the lid as calmly as he could in this heated moment. "Bend over my darling," he whispered tenderly in her ear, as he carefully rolled her dress up and slowly pulled down her lacy, silk knickers.

And so began his affair with a transsexual.

Silvia successfully completed her operation and gender transformation two months later.

Dr McCreigh felt that he had the best of both worlds with Silvia. She was now a woman but because she had been a man she knew exactly how to please a man. She was better than any woman he had ever been with. It was hot, intense passion, which often left him feeling ashamed at the depths of his lust for her.

He couldn't complain about his life with Vanessa because she was a wonderful woman, beautiful, patient and kind and they had a good relationship in all aspects. It was just that being with Silvia was different. He felt saucy and naughty with Silvia and his heart lifted every time he looked forward to their rendezvous. Sometimes he would smile in his office at home, just thinking of all the pleasurable times they spent together. Then afterwards he would feel a sinking sense of guilt because he had a good and faithful wife who tried to please him in every way. Then he started to loathe himself. Then his mobile would bleep and it would be a text message from Silvia, who had the codename "Dr Brompton." His heart would skip a beat and he would make his excuses and leave his happy home to end up in a passionate clinch with Silvia less than 10 miles away.

Dr McCreigh, as well as being a GP, had another string to his professional bow. He was a police doctor. He was on call at certain times of the month to certify deaths and issue death certificates, usually for grisly murders. He had seen it all before and was quite unfazed at the abuse of the human form that he came upon in the course of this duty. The job paid well, although it was antisocial hours and he worked on a roster with other doctors. Financial cutbacks meant that he could be called out all over London.

This weekend he was on duty. Vanessa was horse-riding with her friends in the countryside and he fully expected he would be called out at some point over the weekend. He was wondering if he could factor in some time with Silvia. He never brought her to his house. He always went round to her place or they booked a room in a local, no-frills hotel, where no-one would know him. Silvia understood that they had to be discreet. He paid for her rent so that she no longer needed to share her home with a flatmate. She enjoyed their shared, snatched moments, whether they were shopping or seeing a show in town or just lying in each other's arms wishing life held no complications and that both were free to live the life they now wanted, without obstacles, and with each other.

Dr McCreigh wore reading glasses and he peered over some papers. He had read "*The Lancet*" and was puzzling over the latest government initiatives about the National Health Service when his mobile went. It was the police. They needed him to attend a murder scene. A young woman in Camden. He sighed as he strode downstairs, put his coat on, picked up his medical bag and headed for the door. "Another waste of a life; someone's daughter, sister, mother – creating more unhappiness for a family." He sighed deeply, pressed the auto-ignition button on his car and pulled out of the gravel driveway.

It was 11:30pm when Dr McCreigh arrived at the murder scene. Flashing blue lights were everywhere. An ambulance was parked nearby and the police had cordoned off the area and were trying to keep back curious onlookers. The chill night air added to the gloomy intensity of the atmosphere as Dr McCreigh approached the police cordon and presented his credentials.

"I'm Detective Inspector Magnus," said a young, stocky man with sandy hair who had stepped forward to shake Dr McCreigh's hand.

"Dr Anthony McCreigh, police doctor," replied Dr McCreigh as he was ushered through the cordon, holding his doctor's bag.

"Ok, what we've got," continued Detective Inspector Magnus, "is the death of a young, white woman. Early 20's, I'd say. Not sure if she's been sexually assaulted, although it seems that way. Her undergarments have been disturbed and were round her ankles and there's bruising to her inner thighs. Looks like definite strangulation, due to the pressure marks on her neck. Not sure how long she's been here but the body seems fairly fresh. We've found her wallet and so we'll be able to id her shortly."

Dr McCreigh knelt beside the body and applied surgical gloves, from within his doctor's bag. The young woman had brunette hair and almond eyes that were still open and staring obliquely into space. Her mouth was contorted, as though she was crying out, but no sound emitted. Apart from the bruising to her neck, there were no apparent signs of violence to the body. No stab wounds that he could see. No blows to the back of the head.

Dr McCreigh took her pulse, although it was obvious that she was deceased. He closed her eyes and glanced along the length of her body. It felt almost intrusive to do so. Her clothing had been disturbed about her lower body and he assumed that she had been sexually assaulted. It was not his duty to voice his assumptions however, so he stood up and removed his surgical gloves. Forensics would establish the finer details. He was here merely to issue the death certificate.

Then he noticed her coat. He jolted.

It was the same one that his daughter, Sophie, had been wearing the last time that she was down from University, from a branded, high-street retailer. He felt sickened and forced the thought from his mind.

"I'll issue the certificate," he said soberly as he walked back towards the ambulance and retrieved the form from his bag and a pen. He handed the completed certificate back to

Detective Inspector Magnus, who escorted him back across the police cordon and said goodbye.

Dr McCreigh sighed deeply as he walked back to his car. His Sophie had worn the same coat and this poor girl was about the same sort of age. It could've been his Sophie. It didn't bear thinking about. What if she had been walking through Camden on that night, wearing that coat? What a waste of a life. A young woman in her prime. What kind of toerag would do such a thing? Usually it was someone known to the victim. Did she know her killer?

He had been to so many of these crime scenes over the years yet it never got any easier to detach yourself from what you had witnessed. Not immediately, anyway. He had learnt how to distract himself. Sometimes though, at a later point in time, he would hear a news story and realise that he had issued the death certificate for the victim, and the circumstances of the death and the state of the body would haunt him for quite a while afterwards.

Back in the comfort of his Mercedes, he put the radio on. He didn't start the engine immediately, just sat motionless in the car. That coat had struck a particular chord with him, making him feel a bond with the victim through the knowledge that his daughter owned the exact, same coat. He sighed deeply. He needed to hear talking, music, anything. He needed to think of something else. Distraction. The image of that poor woman lying sprawled out in the bushes on this bleak November night was embedded within his mind. He closed his eyes and visualised it. He couldn't get it out of his mind. An upbeat and chirpy early Beatles song played on the radio. It didn't sufficiently distract him. He switched the radio channel to Radio 4. A play was on. It sounded interesting; a kitchen-sink drama. It still didn't distract him sufficiently, though.

His thoughts kept returning to the crime scene. What had that poor girl been thinking during her final moments. Had she been in agony? Why? This one wasn't the worst that he had seen, and yet, she seemed young. He thought for a moment of his own daughters and then he shuddered. He'd never have made a good pathologist, he semi-smiled ironically to himself. Then he reached for his mobile phone and dialled Silvia's number.

"Darling, are you free this evening? Could I come round? If you could have some brandy on stand-by, that'd be great. Just done a death certificate for a young woman. Murder victim. Not the worst I've seen but …so young, so beautiful." His voice tailed off.

"Don't worry darling, of course you can come round. Will you be staying over?"

"Yes, I could," Dr McCreigh continued, "Vanessa's away this weekend, but I am on call for the police."

"That's ok, sweetie", replied Silvia, "you come round and I'll have a large brandy waiting for you and I will put on something silky and sexy to cheer you up."

Dr McCreigh smiled, the image fixed in his mind now was that of his naughty lover and although he wasn't really feeling particularly romantic, he started the ignition. The Radio 4 play distracted him sufficiently. The freezing night air had chilled the outside windscreen of his luxury car, causing him to turn up the heating to defrost it. He reversed away from the murder scene, setting off for Ealing in expectation of lifting his sombre mood, with some alcohol and in Silvia's loving embrace.

CHAPTER 3

Jebson Dunsmore, known as Jeb, was a local lad of 15. He was 5"9 and of stocky build. He had thin, mousey brown hair and average looks. Being a teen he was prone to some spots, mood swings and aggression. His voice had broken and was quite deep. He loved playing PlayStation games and watching dvds in his room. He had football posters on the walls and pictures of topless women from babe magazines.

Jeb lived on the 10th floor of the Holmville Estate with his mum, June. The view over London was sick. The only good thing about their flat. Jeb never knew his dad who had left his mum before he was born. He had no extended family. Jeb's mum worked hard to make sure they had the bare essentials. Over the years she had held down a string of poorly-paid jobs: a supermarket cashier, an assistant in a hairdresser's and recently she had qualified as a bus driver. He was greatly embarrassed about this. All his mates teased him mercilessly.

"Mum – all female bus drivers are f-ing dykes you know!" he would chide her regularly. Yet he knew that she wasn't a dyke. He had grown up trying to shout out the sound of her cries of passion through the thin walls of their apartment, and remembering the various men that she had brought home. It wasn't uncommon to wake up and find a strange man at the breakfast table. Jeb felt angry about this and he bottled it up. His dad should be at the breakfast table. His dad should be with his mum, and with him. He burned with rage. He clenched his fists and slammed the door on the way out, kicking his school bag in anger. None of her relationships seemed to last. One of the men said she had a "difficult son" and he couldn't cope with it. Silently Jeb was pleased. He didn't want his mum to settle with anyone. Serve the bitch right for shagging around like that. Didn't she have any respect? Fucking whore. Sometimes women were just useless, stupid, dumb fucks.

Jeb hung out with kids from his school who mainly lived on his estate. Finn, a skinny Irish white dude with a very fit older sister, Tiny, handsome, mixed race and with a lot of attitude, all of it bad. Everyone looked up to him. Marcus, athletic, black guy into the latest drum and bass sounds. Tiny's older brother, Julius, was always in and out of prison. "It's a fucking racist state, blud!" he would spit out in disgust. He was part of Big Earl's crew, who were all older and rumour had it, handled guns. Everyone feared them. The older gangs on the estate handed out justice with knives, guns, fists and dealt in drugs. They fought gangs from other estates and each other. Everyone feared Big Earl's crew. They had a bloodthirsty reputation.

Some of the girls of the group were Casey, a white girl with shoulder-length auburn hair and rather skinny, Gemma, also white, with dyed blonde hair, a bit on the tubby side and desperate for male attention. She'd do anyone a sexual favour if it made her more popular. Jeb had found out, to his delight, that this was quite useful. Shireen was black and best friends with Gemma. She was introverted, almost shy. Her mum and Jeb's mum used to work together in the hairdressers. Now her mum worked in a care home, "Wipin' old people's arses, innit? Nasty, man, plain nasty!" She was very resentful, having to look after her two younger brothers when all she wanted to be doing was be getting with Marcus whom she had a huge crush on, but was too shy to show him how much.

They were all in a postcode gang. No-one from the other local estates had better cross the Holmville Estate or they'd get jacked, man. That was the code. You had to protect your area – your yard. It was your honour. Last week a kid from the Ralston Estate had accidentally cycled through the Holmville. He'd been jacked. Shouldn'ta done it, shouldn't have set foot on the Holmville. Would never set foot on the Holmville again. That's the way it went, blud. This ends is our ends.

Everyone spoke *Jafaican*; white kids like Jeb, mixed race kids, black kids and Asian kids. It was the cool way to talk, innit. The dress code was low batties or trackie bottoms, trainers and hooded tops and/or baseball caps and creps. You could customise the look with gold chain bling and gold rings as big as knuckle dusters. A fake diamante earring made you look as cool as a Premiership footballer. The look gave you a sense of power, man. The smaller kids ran scared in front of Jeb and his mates. Made Jeb laugh, "The little shits!" he would shout after them as they fled.

Jeb wasn't shy about having sex, or very choosy about whom he slept with. He was 14 when he'd first done it. Last year. With some girl from school, actually at school, in the toilets. He'd had loadsa girls since then. Lately he was kind of seeing Ashlee, a beautiful mixed race girl, with the kind of attitude that made her more of a challenge, but she was also a bit of a sket and was rumoured to put it about with a few guys. She wasn't part of his crew but she was always hanging round the swings in the playground area and he'd noticed she had a very shapely arse. She seemed to always be "up for it" if he wanted some, and best of all, she knew where to score some top quality weed.

It was a Thursday evening and Jeb, Tiny and Marcus were walking back from the local fish and chip shop, eating as they walked.

They approached the estate.

"Wanna come back to me crib and check out some porn? Me rent won't be back for ages. Driving the late night bus" spat Jeb.

"It's a man's job, innit" giggled Marcus.

"Shut it!" said Jeb, angrily, throwing Marcus a filthy look.

"Safe," they replied, grinning and nudging each other. They all knew how wound up Jeb got about his mum being a bus driver.

"Hey my mains, I joined Tinder this week – check this out," laughed Tiny, lightening the atmosphere and holding up his smartphone.

"Safe, bruv. Whoa – look at that, is that her coochie on show?" laughed Tiny.

They were gathered round Tiny's phone ogling the range of female, some of them naked, hook-ups.

"She's buff," sighed Marcus as they peered at the photo of a very shapely woman's log-in details.

"I ain't never tried dis, but it looks so sick," laughed Tiny in excitement, "I could be bare into this."

"It's quite hype, innit?" said Jeb, suitably impressed and making a mental note to download the app and install it on his phone.

They all smiled. As they neared the estate they bumped into some of the girls. Casey, Shamis, a beautiful, Somalian girl who had dyed pink and black hair and piercings all over her body. She had rebelled in such a way that her family had disowned her and she'd been placed with a foster family. Lucinda was half -English, half-Chinese and always spaced out. Rumour had it she'd been sexually abused by her father and used drugs as a means of escape from a life of little value.

"Hey boys, you up for it?" shouted Casey. The girls giggled. The boys had been challenged. If they refused, they were "gay". Jeb felt angry at being suckered into something he didn't particularly want to do. He would much rather be watching US porn star Edison Fern who held a fascination for him as he watched her skills with various phallic-shaped objects while dressed as a nurse/French maid/policewoman, etc, before male porn star, Bright Gibson, who was massively endowed, would take charge of matters. Their website was very popular with teenage lads.

Yes, Jeb wasn't in the mood for the silly chatter of the local girls' company but felt compelled to shout, "What ya offerin', you bare chirpsing us?"

"Chirpsing?" Shamis laughed, "Whatever you wanna be taking - our amazing booty is all yours."

Jeb turned to his mates, "What say you?" he asked in an undertone. The guys were disappointed. They'd all been building themselves up for an evening watching the very flexible antics of Edison Fern and Bright Gibson.

"Come on don't be pussies" shouted Casey, "this offer will soon be withdrawn like your lame dicks" she laughed.

"That was deep!" shouted Marcus.

"You just beggin' now! I ain't never got a lame dick!" replied Tiny, taking the initiative and striding towards the girls.

"So," he drawled as he slipped an arm round Shamis "you got bare piercings everywhere? And I mean *everywhere*?" he enquired.

Shamis giggled and nodded.

"Well, I wanna get wiv you then, babe and check 'em out, know what I mean?" he replied, running his free hand over her bottom and winking at Jeb and Marcus.

Shamis giggled. Everyone thought Tiny was so cool.

"Let's go somewhere more private and leave these yute behind, you get me?" he laughed, leading her towards the canal towpath, which was shady and overgrown. Shamis giggled as they set off, with Tiny whispering obscenities into her ear. She felt like a star. She felt like a million dollars. Everyone knew Tiny was so sexy and he had chosen her. It was an honour.

"He's got the gift, innit?" spat Jeb with more than a little envy.

"Well?" shouted Casey straight at him.

"Yeah, alright, alright babe, but I'm kinda wid Ashlee, you know and .." Jeb stopped when he saw Casey's face darken.

"What? You wouldn't wanna get wiv me cos of dat sket?" she shouted angrily. "You know she goes wiv every main. Last week she was getting with Big Earl!"

"No, no, babes. Dat's not what I is saying. Hear me out. You're bare sick, so allow it, I is nuff sorry, innit. Let's start over, come on babe" he said, and, feeling that he had done enough to reassure her, he strode purposefully over to her, throwing the empty fish and chips box onto the path.

Meanwhile Lucinda and Marcus looked disinterestedly at each other. "I gonna split, blud," said Marcus with a shrug. "Bare tings to do, innit," he justified as he walked away. He'd go home and watch some porn alone. It would be better because he could have a long, slow "me time" while watching it. His parents wouldn't be home for ages. He smiled to himself.

Lucinda popped a pill into her mouth and continued silently gazing into space. She set off on the path towards the entrance to her block on the Holmville, walking slowly and hallucinating about giant purple and green shapes as she went and the music inside her head was as fast and furious as the shapes that danced before her in time with the beat.

Jeb and Casey were sitting on the grass, deeply engrossed in each other, kissing and groping and oblivious to the outside world. "What you fucking staring at?" roared Jeb, suddenly breaking from Casey's kiss as he spotted a middle aged couple walking past and tutting. "I'm gonna go over and fucking smack 'em one," he continued, about to stand up, while Casey held his head in her hands and tried to regain his focus. "Babe, allow it! They ain't worth it babe. Just allow," she continued. She could sense his rage. He seemed to get fired up at the least little thing. She sensed that she was losing his focus, so she rubbed a firm hand across his groin and his gaze was instantly upon her again. He ran his hand up her thigh. "Uhm" he murmured as they continued kissing and slinked into the shadows at the back of the estate, where the dustbins were.

Suddenly Jeb grabbed hold of Casey and pinned her down roughly on the ground, amidst the broken glass bottles and the stray bags of rubbish.

Jeb ripped open her shirt and roughly grabbed at her breasts.

"Hey!" she shouted, "What the fuck you doin?"

He pressed his full body weight upon her, looked down at her powerless beneath him and smiled. He realised that he was taking things too far, however, he enjoyed feeling her body wriggle in fear under the weight of his.

"Sorry, babe, I was just getting too into it, you know? You is so hot! Sorry, if I was rough. You're so fit, you know. You turn me on too much."

His words seemed to reassure her as he felt her body relax and she began to kiss him again.

Ten minutes later, Jeb emerged from the dustbin area, tucking his t-shirt into his jeans, his head was aching but he felt content. He felt calm. That was nang! Casey had been so good. He'd never had her before, but he would do her again, if she was up for it. He was grinning from ear to ear. Casey seemed to have enjoyed it too. She'd been panting and gyrating and egging him on as she cried out at the end. He was quite surprised and very embarrassed. He didn't know what to think about Ashlee though. He didn't much care for her, after hearing Casey say that Ashlee had got with Big Earl. He certainly didn't want to think about that right now because it would deflate his mood.

He'd scored. He was "The Man". He felt 10ft tall. Jeb headed straight off in the direction of home. He trod on a snail on the path and enjoyed squashing it to a pulp.

Casey emerged shortly after him buttoning up her shirt and adjusting her skimpy skirt. She glanced both ways to check that she hadn't been seen and ran off in the direction of the car park, which led through to the entrance way to her flat on the Holmville.

Mrs Molson, making tea at her kitchen window, saw the young couple in various stages of undress, emerging from the dustbins area. She tutted and muttered to herself about a lack of Christian values in young people these days as she took down the biscuit tin and helped herself to a Digestive biscuit.

Runi Lancel, aged 27, and with a solid gold tooth, was employed by a national crime prevention organisation which was joint funded by the local council. He was a youth worker.

Runi was tasked with running the Midnight Basketball crime prevention initiative on the Holmville Estate. The Youth Centre was a pokey, run-down building. It had boarded up windows, graffitied walls and smelled bad. It was dusty and grimy inside. Runi, with his team of volunteers, had cleaned the place up, laid down the markings for basketball, brought in two basketball nets, and produced posters advertising Midnight Basketball. His genuine, driven enthusiasm and conviction in what he was doing rubbed off on everyone who met him. He exuded charm and a can-do attitude.

He wanted his team from the Holmville Estate to join the Midnight Basketball League, and possibly win the cup one year. He wanted the local youths to succeed in the way that he had. He understood them. He had a genuine passion for what he did.

After all, he'd grown up on the Invicta Estate in south London, near Elephant and Castle. He'd once been involved with gun-running and drug couriering as a youth. The youngest of a family of six, his muscular physique gave the impression of physical toughness. He used to go to the local, council-run gym to build up muscle fitness. He needed to look "hard."

The gang he was in, "the JT's" - Jamaica Tigers - encouraged its senior members to get a particular tattoo to prove their membership and loyalty. You had to be Jamaican or have a family heritage from Jamaica to join. Runi's mum was Jamaican and that was enough to gain entry. Runi was very proud when the Jamaican flag with a tiger superimposed over it was tattooed into his upper arm. "Like a yardie!" he thought. His arm muscles were so tight that having the tattoo done was a virtually painless experience.

Ewan, the skinny gothic tattooist wore his long, dyed black, hair tied back. He had nose and mouth piercings and tattoos up both arms. Ewan knew not to ask questions when young black men asked for this particular tattoo. He'd heard rumours that it was a gang emblem but he deliberately showed no interest in it. He never spoke as he worked. There was no point in trying to make conversation with these gang youths. They didn't have anything to say and they probably loathed the heavy rock anthems that pounded from the shop's speakers. Ewan soothed his conscience at undertaking such work by repeating the mantra that he just wanted to earn money from his craft. It didn't take long to ink the tattoo. Pretty soon the job was done, the client had paid and no questions were asked.

Ewan shut it out of his mind. Post-tattooing these guys, he always had a cigarette, in the side alley, to calm his nerves. Today he decided to go for a piss first and then have a smoke. He was oblivious to the fact that his tattoo parlour was under surveillance by a rival gang who had discovered that he tattooed members of the Jamaica Tigers gang.

Under the overcast, routinely grey London skies, Runi strode out of the tattoo parlour with a grin on his face. He felt as though the tattoo burning into his arm was visible through his t-shirt sleeves, which, of course, it wasn't. Whilst immersed in his thoughts, he never even noticed that two shady characters were watching him from across the street. With a hand gesture from one to the other, they suddenly broke into a sprint in Runi's direction, seized him by the arms and led him to the side alley that adjoined the tattoo parlour, where they gave him a severe and vicious beating, causing him to lose one of his front teeth.

It was at precisely that moment that Ewan had stepped gingerly into the alley to have his post-tattooing fag. He heard a commotion and, looking up, saw the young lad that he'd just tattooed getting quite a beating from two, thick-set men in baggy jeans with knuckle duster gold rings and chains, and in sport hoodies. They were laying into the young guy big time and seemed intent on even killing him.

"Tell us, ya fucker," one of the gang cried, as the blows and kicks rained down on Runi, "When's the next crack load arriving?"

Runi remembered the gang motto, "Never say, never tell, take the beats, laters we send 'em to hell!" It was engrained in his psyche. He maintained his silence and, apart from coughing up blood, and the occasional groan, he emitted no sound.

Ewan retreated silently into the shop and gently bolted the door behind him. Then he took his mobile out and dialled 999.

The Lovell Street Gang were getting nothing out of Runi. "Fuck, let's split!" one of them shouted as he saw a police officer making his way down the alley. They fled at speed and Runi lifted his beaten and bloodied body from the floor. It was difficult standing up. His ribs ached, one of his eyes was closed and he felt blood on his face. His blood-soaked t-shirt was torn to shreds.

"Are you alright, son?" asked the police officer. He noticed the tattoo of the Jamaica Tigers gang on Runi's arm, peering through the bloodstained remains of what had once been a sports t-shirt, and realised that this youth was most likely not going to tell him anything. Runi eyed the policeman with his one, opened eye, "Yeah," he groaned. His mouth filled with blood. "I'm fine," but then he slumped to the ground and blacked out.

The sound of medical equipment and the noise of general chatter entered Runi's consciousness. Runi opened his eyes. His mother sat weeping by his bedside. She was holding his hand. "Praise Jesus, you're ok!" she exclaimed. She was quite a theatrical personality, always making a drama out of the least thing.

"What happened 'bro?" asked one of his brothers, seated next to their mother.

Runi realised he was in hospital. "Eh?" he said. He tried to remember. He ached. He felt sore.

"The doctor told us you suffered two broken ribs and a fractured eye socket. You're very lucky that you wasn't more badly hurt. You've had concussion."

"Son, son, I love you, son," his mother cried, tearfully. She clasped his hands. "We've been praying for you in church. The pastor even said a special prayer last Sunday." She realised that Runi wasn't taking in anything she was saying. He was looking over her shoulder at the tall, smartly dressed figure of Raydon Darnell, who had appeared as if out of nowhere.

"Hey, Raydon," said Runi's brother with total admiration and reverence, "How ya doin, man?" He shook Raydon's hand vigorously.

With his other hand, Raydon removed his Ray-ban sunglasses, slowly, deliberately. He placed them in the top pocket of his Giorgio Armani, sleek leather jacket. His solid gold Rolex Daytona watch glinted in the sunlight from the ward window situated behind Runi's bed.

Raydon turned towards Shakeel, Runi's brother. "I'm good, Shakeel. I'm good." He smiled and kissed Runi's mother's free hand, the bristles of his goatee beard causing her to blush and smile broadly. "Mrs Lancel," he said, politely acknowledging her.

She smiled politely back.

"Mum, why don't we come back and see Runi tomorrow?" said Shakeel, guiding his mother up out of the chair, sensing that Raydon wanted to talk to Runi alone.

"Ok, see you tomorrow son," she said, "I'll keep praying to the sweet Lord Jesus," she kissed Runi's forehead, gave him a comforting smile and left the hospital ward, arm in arm with Shakeel, chattering joyously to him.

Raydon, glanced around, saw no-one of note, and drew the cubicle curtain around Runi's bed. He pulled up a chair and sat close to Runi.

"Runi, bruv," he said, "Yas done good, blud. Yas said nutin. Yas ma' main."

Runi tried to smile, but his face ached.

"Ya missin' a tooth? No worries," continued Raydon "me dentist gonna fix ya up with a solid gold toof. Me way of a thank you."

"Really?" the 20-year old Runi was very impressed and in awe.

"Yes, yes, we're cool on dat. When you out of here, call Dr Ahmed, he sort it for you, no charge. Solid gold bro, can you believe that? Bare solid gold, bruv" Raydon chuckled. He knew how these younger guys were impressed by gold, designer items and the symbols of wealth.

Runi felt obliged to laugh in response, to make Raydon feel pleased and appreciated. After all, he'd seen Raydon use a pistol to shoot a man in the head. Brains splattered everywhere. Raydon didn't mess with anyone and anyone with any sense shouldn't mess with Raydon.

"Now listen," said Raydon, and he drew so close to Runi that Runi could smell the garlic on his breath, "I got work for you, after you outta here and fixed your tooth and I'm gonna sort ya with a piece. You know how to use one?"

Runi nodded because his face felt so sore that talking was difficult. He was worried. He didn't want to possess a gun, let alone be in situations where he'd need to use one. He figured out that by taking this beating, he had moved up the rung of gang status to a higher level of trust.

"I got a shipment coming in. You know that one of my chain of milkshake bars - the London Bridge one? Shipment of ice cream, ya get me, is gonna arrive. Pure, ice-cream. Top quality. Nang. You is to take delivery. And then let me know and I get me generals to move it to da crack house, on Featherstone Street, our ends, innit. Ya understand. Ya get me?"

Runi felt real fear, for the first time in his life. He nodded.

"Good boi," said Raydon, standing up. He placed a £50 note on the bedside table next to Runi's glass of water.

Raydon pointed at the money as he stood by the cubicle curtain. "Buy yerself some porn dvds, and ciggies or somefink, innit." He laughed as he drew open the cubicle curtain, paused, and then looked back at the incredulous Runi.

"Can't be on de long ting. Ya let me know when ya outta here. Oh, I forgot to tell you. Lovell Street Gang got jacked. Two of dem in hospital – not this hospital. Score is settled. Karma is a wonderful ting." He headed towards the ward exit laughing still.

Runi lay rooted to the bed in fear. He knew that he was involved in something much deeper than he had imagined or ever wanted. He'd been beaten before, but not as severely as this. Not enough to land him in hospital. He was afraid. He wanted out. He wanted to rip that nasty tattoo out of his skin. The beating he'd received had brought home to him the truth that he probably wouldn't get out of the gang alive. Would he even be able to get away? Would he have to have plastic surgery and a new identity to live a free life? Could he ever own his own home, or have a family? He had no education, as such. He could read and write and do simple sums. He'd never thought of these things before. The gang had meant everything to him. If he left, his family would be in danger and he'd be dead. What to do?

Runi turned his sore, bandaged head, towards the £50 note on the table. He didn't want it. He didn't want any part of it. A solid gold tooth would be cool though.

CHAPTER 4

Maya Fullbright was brushing her long, lush, brunette hair in front of the mirror in the bathroom. She was 23. On completion of her university degree in English and Economics she was finding it hard to get a job and move out of home. Countless applications had brought countless rejections. It was demoralising. Yet, she wouldn't give up. She was determined to get an entry-level administration job in human resources and then undertake the necessary qualifications to progress further in her chosen field and make a long term career out of it.

She lived with her parents in a small, terraced house in Fulham. Her parents were elderly, having had her late in life. Her mother, Tessa, had had problems conceiving and when she finally fell pregnant at the age of 42 they were both thrilled and overwhelmed. Her father, Harold, was a retired civil engineer. He loved gardening and pottered about planting various seedlings in their back garden. He loved pottering his garden shed, in their small, suburban garden.

"My own country getaway!" he would laugh.

Being an only child, Maya's parents doted on her and were chuffed to bits and thrilled to pieces when she completed her degree, even though they had been the eldest parents at the graduation ceremony, and were mistaken for her grandparents. A large, silver-framed photo of Maya in her cap and gown took pride of place on the living room table.

Maya had gorgeous white teeth that completed a beautifully-aligned, perfect smile. It was what was considered a "Hollywood" smile. She dazzled all who met her. Socially she went out with her uni friends. She didn't have a serious boyfriend and that didn't bother her, as she was in no rush to settle down. Although, she had been seeing Ryan Quinn, during her final year of University.

Ryan was an athletic and charming guy always, punctual, always on time. He had even met her parents on one of her term breaks.

"Such a lovely chap, that Ryan," her mum had said afterwards.

From time to time her mother would ask, "How's that friend of yours, Ryan, doing?"

Maya's heart would sink. She had looked up to Ryan and he had been her world for the final year of her studies. They had been inseparable. They would study together, go to lunch together and sleep over at each other's student digs. Yet as soon as university was over, he had ditched her. Just like that. Without warning. She was deeply hurt.

He had returned to London and, from what she could gather from seeking out his LinkedIn profile, he was a trainee Markets Analyst at a top City Bank. From his Facebook profile it was apparent that he was "in a relationship" with Susie-Jane Rustin, whoever she was. Maya quickly realised that she had just been convenient company for him while he was studying.

She had felt so raw about it when it was over but hadn't dwelt on it for too long, particularly when she realised that he was now seeing someone else. It helped her to move on. So, when her mother asked her about Ryan, it irritated her.

"I'm not really in touch with him anymore," Maya would reply.

"Pity. He seemed such a nice chap," her mother would reply and Maya wouldn't add anything further. Her mother never pushed it any further and the conversation would end at that point.

While waiting for that career break that would finally launch her, Maya held down a part-time job as a barrista in a chain coffee house in their Camden High Street branch, for which she was paid the minimum wage. She earnt enough to feel independent from her elderly parents, even though she couldn't afford to move out. Her employers provided her with a uniform for the job, which consisted of a shirt with her name badge and dark trousers. She was trained up on the equipment, which wasn't too mentally demanding. Apparently she could whip up a mean mochaccino with marshmallows and froth.

Although her job wasn't intellectually stimulating or her first step to a future career, at least she earned some money with which to pay some rent to her parents and run her second-hand, run down small car. Maya never drove to work though as it was difficult to park and, being far from home, the cost of petrol would have been too high, in relation to her salary.

"One day I will get the job that I deserve and make my parents proud," she would tell herself while working the till, stamping the customer loyalty cards and handing the hot drinks over to the customers. Until then, she would have to content herself with dazzling her beautiful smile at customers, while they waited in line for their coffees.

"Yo, blud, it's dem ragheads," spat Marcus, nudging Jeb as they walked, with Finn and Tiny, along a walkway on the Holmville that ran alongside the canal. School was over for the day and Marcus had rolled the largest spliff Jeb had ever seen and they were gonna go and have a relaxing smoke in their favourite spot in the overgrowth, down by the canal.

"Assalum aleikum, bruvers."

Jeb and his mates looked up. "It's that jackass, Ahmed, and his crew. Shit," mumbled Jeb under his breath.

Ahmed Mirwani and his friends, Abdul Mutal Barija and Zohair Dasti, all wore traditional shalwar kameez, sported beards of varying lengths and wore taqiyah, Muslim skullcaps, on their heads. They were all British born, of Pakistani heritage and had recently become very religious, following a short stint in prison. The imam of their local mosque was a charismatic speaker who had gained their trust and inspired them to be the best Muslims that they could be. They were carrying leaflets for the street stand that they manned on the high street, where they did dawah – trying to encourage people to convert to Islam. "Bring people to the faith," the imam had encouraged them, "Show them by example. Be patient and tolerant."

Ahmed shouted out at the dishevelled looking bunch of lads in front of him. "Where you heading?"

"Goin' for a walk," replied Finn, unconvincingly, putting his hands into his baggy jeans pocket and shrugging, "but bit of a random question, Ahmed."

"Ha, bruvers, come and learn about Islam with me. It's the fastest growing religion in the UK, innit. Islam will put you back on the right path, bruvvers."

Stoney faces and silence met Ahmed's enthusiastic endorsements.

"Bruvvers, it changed my life", Ahmed continued, "I was into drugs, women, bad tings. When I was banged up, the imam come to see me, we talked. He explained in depth the Quran and about Allah's prophet, prophet Muhammed, peace be upon him, and it's changed my life, man, I swear."

"Ahmed, I like kebabs, I do and I've probably eaten Halal burgers in that burger shop on the high street, but I ain't into religion, sorry bro. I don't believe in dat shit. That goes for any religion, not just your one" stated Marcus. His deep voice gave him that extra air of authority and conviction.

"We'll do dawah elsewhere," Ahmed said in a quieter voice to his two friends, who nodded.

Ahmed raised his voice. "Listen, anytime you bruvvers want to turn your lives around, remember, we can help," he said in sincerity, as he and his friends moved on, posters and leaflets tucked under their arms, as they headed towards the passageway that led from the estate to the high street.

"Nah, we're alright thanks," shouted Jeb arrogantly after them. His mates were giggling and he felt emboldened, "going to get high now and shagged laters!" Jeb grabbed at his crotch mockingly and his mates were now giggling loudly.

"That one's a complete bastard," stated Ahmed in a low voice to his two friends who nodded in agreement as they walked even further away. "Allah will have no mercy on his soul. The fires of hell await that filthy kuffar."

"More than the others?" asked Abdul Mutal, earnestly.

"Oh yeah," said Ahmed with a smirk, "much more," as they walked past the heavily graffitied walls of the narrow passageway that led out onto the high street.

Maya was nervous. She finally had an interview at a recruitment company in the City of London. She took a deep breath. Apparently, RM3 Recruitment had liked her application form and her LinkedIn profile, and had invited her for an online assessment. After passing the test, she had undertaken a telephone interview. She had passed that with flying colours and was now invited to a face-to-face interview. She'd hardly dared to tell her parents, who were gushing with pride and hope for her.

"Sweetie, have you got a good outfit?" asked her mum. "This could be your big break."

"Of course," she replied, "I bought this suit." She opened her wardrobe and brought out a dark blue suit, which she would match up with a crisp, white shirt and a pastel coloured pashmina.

"Oh, it's beautiful. Lucky you're so slim and can get away with wearing anything," giggled her mum.

"I know," Maya replied, "apparently I take after my mum." They both laughed.

"What about these shoes?" Maya brought out a high heeled pair of navy shoes.

"Are you sure you'll be comfortable in those?" questioned her mother, "You don't want to trip over. It would make a terrible first impression."

They were very close. Maya was the pride and joy of her parents.

"I'll wear these." Maya brought a more sensible pair of camel coloured shoes out of her wardrobe.

Down by the canal side, hidden in the long grass, Jeb and his mates passed a large spliff around.

"Feeling chilled?" giggled Marcus, "I am just lying here, jammin wid me bruds. How sick is dat?"

Jeb lay back and looked up at the sky. He felt peaceful.

"Mmmm," he said. His senses felt heightened and distorted.

Every tweet from every bird was amplified in sound, the bees

buzzing through the long grass sounded like violin strings in

an orchestra. He giggled.

"Pass it to me" said Finn agitatedly.

Tiny took a long slow draw on the joint and passed it to Finn,

whilst exhaling smoke rings.

"Dat is so nang" remarked Marcus. "Innit nang, though?"

Tiny laughed.

Jeb felt sleepy. "Are the girls coming to the yard?" he asked.

"Aw, man, all you tinkin' about is shagging, man!" stated

Marcus.

"Yeah, course I am," laughed Jeb.

Finn was giggling.

"Pass, pass, man. Come on, you had it for ages" Jeb said to Finn, slightly aggressively.

"Awright, awright," said Finn, handing it to Jeb, who snatched it from his grip.

"And don't be too long," said Marcus, "because I haven't had some for ages."

"Oooh, you ain't had any for ages!" laughed Finn, mockingly.

Jeb exhaled, smiling and passed the joint to Marcus.

"Oh, fuck off man. I wasn't talking about pussy," retorted Marcus, somewhat annoyed, taking a drag on the joint.

"Lately, I been doin' it without a rubber," stated Jeb.

"Say what?" said Finn, completely shocked.

"Hey, blud be careful, bro," said Marcus with genuine concern, "As far as I is concerned, no glove, no love," he laughed.

"Yolo!!!" laughed Jeb, "It feels so much better, and dat reminding me, where dem bitches? Are they comin' to da yard, cos I wanna get me some, ya get me?"

"Oh bro, I told them to be here at 5. Didn't wanna share the spliff with dems. Less for us, ya get me?" said Tiny.

"Safe," said Marcus, passing what was left of the joint to Tiny, and putting his MP3 player onto loud speaker. Drum and Bass sounds pounded from its speaker.

The last puff of the joint went to Finn. They were all high as kites now and waiting for the girls to show. They lazed about in a dreamlike state. Jeb drifted off to sleep. Tiny traced his name in the earth and smiled constantly. Marcus stood up and danced in time to the beat.

"Yo, where's dem babes?" asked Finn at 5.30pm.

"Dunno," shrugged Tiny. He was feeling pretty hungry. "Does anyone else wanna get a kebab from the Turkish?"

"Fuckin' skets must be doing someone else. Probs it's big Earl and his crew," spat Marcus in disgust.

That woke Jeb up.

"Skets!!" shouted Jeb, punching the ground. It hurt. "Ow, that fuckin' hurt!" he cried out.

Marcus started laughing uncontrollably, which set the mood for all of them to have the giggles.

"Wanna come back to mine and watch some porn then, or play FIFA? Me rents be out til laters," asked Finn.

"Rather get me some real flesh, you know what I'm sayin'?" said Jeb.

"Yeah but there ain't any, Jeb" protested Finn.

"Let's split," said Marcus, "it's getting cold and I got me homework to do."

"I can't believe you still do that school shit. You ain't gonna get no job at the end," said Tiny.

"Yeah, but electronics is me ting, innit, so if I get a bare couple of GCSE's I might get an apprenticeship as an electrician."

"Fuckin' school swat! Allow for school," chided Jeb, laughing.

"Man, if you get an electronics GCSE, you'll be in some factory making vibrators or sometin''" laughed Tiny and they all dissolved into fits of giggles and set off in different directions to their respective flats on the Holmville Estate, and the kebab shop.

Jeb put the key into his front door and walked in. As usual, his mum wasn't home and the place was a tip. There was a note on the table.

"*Hi darling, working late tonight. Doing an extra shift. Here's a tenner, go and get yerself a pizza or a burger and chips. Love mum x*"

Jeb sniffed, and wiped his snotty nose on the sleeve of his hoodie. He pocketed the tenner, opened the fridge and downed half a pint of milk straight from the carton. He was looking to build up his strength and had been going to the local council-run gym a lot. He'd got a student discount card, which meant that he only paid £2 each time he went. He loved weight training and the running machine. He got an adrenaline high from it. He tried to go three times a week after school. He had wanted to bulk up like a WWF fighter. He looked at his increasingly muscular arms in the bathroom window and smiled to himself.

CHAPTER 5

On the day of the interview, Maya's father kissed her forehead and wished her luck.

"Darling, I know you're going to do well," he said.

"Maya," her mum called after her, "Maya, don't forget to smile."

"I won't," replied Maya and she headed off to the tube station.

Maya stepped out of Cannon Street tube station, amongst the bustling crowds of commuters, and took a deep breath to steady her nerves. It was the day of her interview. She was early. She'd noted the company's address and planned her route. She was happy with her time-keeping, as she didn't like living on the edge and wouldn't wish to arrive in a sweaty, dishevelled heap.

Being early, she decided to stop for a cup of coffee in one of the main chain coffee shops that proliferated the streets of the City. They were all similarly anodyne and she didn't have a particular preference for any one of them. On entering the nearest one, she scanned the sandwiches and salads on display and was jostled by busy City workers manoeuvring into the surrounding space, negotiating ready-made porridge and various hot beverages. The place was busy and buzzing with atmosphere. Maya felt that she would come here at lunchtimes, if her job application was successful.

"£3.95," said the counter assistant in Polish-accented English. Maya smiled and handed over a £5 note. She was relieved that she wasn't working tonight. She knew what it was like to serve people from behind a counter and was glad to be free of it for one night.

"There you go," continued the assistant, handing over the change, amid the busy hustle and bustle of the coffee shop.

Maya found a table and sat down. She mentally rehearsed her answers to standard interview questions. Job interviews were such a game. She wondered why people had to play this game, answering silly questions such as where one expects to be in 5 years' time, or 'what are your strengths and weaknesses?' She had practiced the methodology of competency-based, STAR interview techniques and had her answers prepared. She knew that the role was highly competitive and that she'd have to be at the top of her game to progress. Interviews were tough these days. London was awash with people, all after these positions, and she wondered if she had some small advantage which would give her the edge over the other, equally qualified applicants.

Keeping a careful eye on the time, she finished her cup of coffee and headed to the toilets, where she reapplied her lipstick and brushed her hair. Then she set off towards the steel and glass structure that was the home of RM3 Recruitment. In the reception area, Maya was made to sign into the visitors book, given a temporary entry pass and escorted to a seat, where she was told her interviewer would come and collect her. Maya sat down and looked around. The building was modern, light and airy. Glass elevators glided up and down and people entered and exited the revolving building entrance doors with great frequency. Maya wondered what it would be like to work here. At that moment, a smartly dressed, older lady appeared and extended a hand.

"Maya Fullbright?" she asked, "I'm Samantha Davis. Do please follow me."

Maya shook Samantha's hand and followed her towards the elevator. Samantha swiped her entry card and the elevator doors opened.

"Did you have far to travel?" asked Samantha in a soothing tone, as the elevator doors closed and their ascent to the 12th floor commenced.

"No, not far. I found it quite easily," replied Maya in awe at the view, as the glass elevator lifted them high above the ground and the City of London was visible through the exterior walls of the elevator.

"It's a spectacular view, isn't it?" said Samantha, who was used to using the standard ice-breaker terminology on interviewees and putting them at their ease.

"Wonderful, yes," replied Maya, smiling.

What a lovely smile, thought Samantha, approvingly. She also liked the interview outfit that Maya was wearing. All in all, she had a positive first impression of this young lady already. Maya was ticking all the right boxes.

The elevator arrived speedily at the 12th floor and they stepped out and headed down the corridor towards the boardroom. Samantha used her entry pass to open the door.

Seated around the large glass table were two other people. Paul Stalton, Head of Human Resources, a man of about 35 years old, who wore a smart suit with an open-necked shirt. He had a harshly wrinkled face, and a day's growth of stubble which made him, somewhat, attractive. The lady seated next to him wore square rimmed glasses and a designer business suit. She seemed older and rather serious. Throughout the interview she rarely smiled or gave off any indication as to whether Maya would be shortlisted. Her name was Jane Riversly and she would be Maya's line manager. Maya thought she was a bit grim, and rather fearsome.

The view of London through the glass window behind them was that of steel and glass towers highlighted against the backdrop of the grey London skies. The brightness of the room's lighting was in contrast to the dull greyness of London beyond them.

Introductions were made, Maya was seated and tea and coffee, with petite four biscuits was served.

Maya took in the view, the atmosphere and mentally summed up and analysed her interviewers. She hid her nerves and set about the interview with a veneer of calmness and intelligence.

The interview commenced. The interviewers used their well-rehearsed questions on Maya. She replied with her well-rehearsed answers, being careful to avoid clichéd words, and used examples, where relevant, which was so important these days, in the competitive London job market. She smiled, nodded and showed keenness at appropriate times in the interview. She also demonstrated that she had researched the firm, used their website and had a few questions of her own to ask her interviewers.

It was hard to tell how she had done, but she felt positive when she left the boardroom, and Samantha escorted her towards the lift and their return to ground level. It was one of the most formal interviews that she had undertaken so far.

Maya decided that she would wait to receive a letter, email or phone call from them and put it out of her mind, for now. It was all good experience, however it had gone. One had to be positive and try not to take it personally. She was used to rejection. One had to move on swiftly. It had been amazing to see London from such a height. She'd never been to New York, or experienced skyscrapers, so going to the 12th floor of a building was literally quite dizzying. The view had made her impressed her and she felt that she would enjoy working there. She so hoped that she had been successful. In the meantime, until she heard from RM3, she would keep applying for other jobs in this field.

As soon as Maya had left the boardroom, Paul Stalton turned towards Jane Riversly, smiling and said, "She's the one, no doubt about it."

"Yes," replied Jane, "I was very impressed. I'm sure she'll integrate into the role very well indeed."

"I don't even think a second interview is necessary," Paul said, finishing his coffee.

"No," Jane agreed. "She was the stand-out candidate. Top notch. We should just send out an offer letter." Paul agreed.

Runi Lancel had told them all that they should get fitter if they wanted to make the grade, and be picked for his Midnight Basketball squad. Runi was an amazing guy. A legend amongst Jeb and his friends and they all wanted to impress him. He had a good understanding of what their life was like.

He was never judgemental. He seemed so genuine. Jeb, in particular, had a real affinity for him.

Jeb went into his room and booted up his computer. His screensaver was a picture of a naked lady, spread-eagled and gagged. It turned Jeb on. He went straight onto the search engine and looked up his favourite rape and sexual violence website. His hand moved down the inside front of his tracksuit bottoms and he became lost in a world of violent pornography and self-stimulation. Lately his internet habits had become more and more extreme. His thought processes were that a "real man" must control a woman; show her who is boss. He'd never let a woman control him. He was certain of that.

It was after school, two days later and Jeb couldn't work out why he wasn't enjoying the snuff movies that he was watching online. He wasn't getting that kick from them that he used to. He had become interested in what is known as "the dark net". He learnt how to access it and went into online chatrooms with deviant people, discussing deviant things. Jeb's nickname was "Camdenmassive". He thought it made him sound tough.

Someone calling themselves "Solster One" was chatting to him. Solster One claimed to be a man of 38 who actually took part in snuff movies. He boasted that he'd raped and killed people. Men and women. Jeb was a little afraid of him and a little in awe.

"You need to get out there and get on with it," Solster One advised Jeb. "No more pussyfooting around, mate. You need to show her who's boss. And you know what? She'll love it. Just give her one, hard and rough. Make it hurt. Make her suffer."

"Really?" asked Camdenmassive. "What like? Actually rape someone?"

"Of course. I'm not mucking about here. Hold her down and fuck her hard. The bitch deserves it."

"But who do I choose? How did you select?"

"YOU'RE AN AMATEUR, AND I AIN'T GOT TIME TO CHAT WITH YA. FUCK OFF WASTING MY TIME!" typed Solster One, in capital letters to give the impression of shouting.

"No, wait .." typed Camdenmassive, but Solster One had left the chatroom.

Jeb heard his mum's key in the front door. He felt cold sweat trickling down his forehead. He quickly exited the dark web, deleted his browsing history and shut down the computer.

"Jeb," called his mum, "Jeb, you in yer room?"

"Yeah," he shouted back, "doing some homework." He smirked to himself.

"Good boy," replied his mum. "I'm on lates tonight. So, I'm gonna leave you some money to get a kebab or a burger. Just popped back from the dry cleaners with me spare uniform. Wasn't sure you'd be in. Anyway, the money's on the table."

Jeb scowled. He couldn't remember the last time she'd been home for supper. She never had supper with him these days because of that bloody job. Fucking bus company. He'd

tagged Camden Massive in very large letters on the back

window of one of their buses on the top deck. He'd go and tag

the whole fleet of them. Fuckers! He had the sketching tools.

"Yeah, ok," replied Jeb, but he clenched his fist and closed his

eyes to mask his anger.

As soon as he heard the front door close, he checked his

watch and went into the kitchen to pocket the £10 that his

mum had left him for his supper. As he did so, he caught sight

of his reflection in the mirror walking into the kitchen. He

stopped to look at himself. He wasn't good-looking in any way.

He had a large mouth, and small, disproportioned eyes. His

nose was average and his skin, slightly spotty. He'd never had

trouble pulling women though. Mind you, the girls round the

Holmville were just horny, young slappers, who'd shag

anything with a pulse. Jeb ran his hand through his hair.

If he was to rape someone, he'd need to get some kit. A balaclava, gloves, a knife. He'd need to go to a sports shop to buy some of it.

Where would he hide it? He knew his mum came into his room to tidy up and hoover. He had a secret place, under his bed, where the carpet was raised and he'd pulled up some flooring to create a hiding place. It was where he kept some porn DVD's and his marijuana. Yeah, he'd keep it in there. She'd never find it there. He'd go and buy it now.

Jeb locked the front door and sauntered to the lift. He had a purpose. He was planning something big. He could end up famous. He laughed at the idea that he could be as famous as Ati Adeofale.

Meanwhile June had arrived, in a breathless rush, at the bus depot wearing her driver's uniform.

"You're late, June, just get the bus out, I'll sign you in!" said her manager, as she ran across the yard towards the bus that she usually drove.

"Not that one, June," he shouted after her, pointing at another bus, "that one. Some bastards have been tagging again and your bus is going for repairs tomorrow morning. If I could catch the scum that waste our time and effort scrawling their shit on the windows …" His voice tailed off.

June's heart sank. She knew that Jeb had a graffiti sketching kit in his room. She'd seen it when she went in there to hoover. She just hoped it wasn't him or his mates. She made a mental note to have a word with him about graffiti and the cost of removing it, when they next had supper together. Then she got cross with herself for even thinking that it might be Jeb. London was a big place with loads of kids. It could be anyone of them. Why did she think badly of him? He was a good boy, wasn't he?

Jeb shuffled to the counter of the sports shop and placed down a balaclava, and ski gloves and a football. He wouldn't be able to buy a knife. He'd just use the kitchen bread knife, he reasoned. He'd wipe all the prints off it first. He was a little proud of his slick thought processes.

"I'm going skiing," he told the checkout girl, unconvincingly, as she looked quizzically at his items, "the football's for my younger brother's birthday," he added.

She half-smiled as he paid her and he left the shop with the items in a bag and no money left for supper.

He was hungry. Tonight was Midnight Basketball try-outs down at the Youth Centre and Runi was always a sucker for a hard luck story. Perhaps he could blag some money off of him and get something for supper. He wondered what Midnight Basketball would be about. He laughed at the name, because it wasn't played at midnight. They were to meet at the youth centre at 8:00pm.

Jeb went home and hid the balaclava and skiing gloves in the hiding place under his bed.

He changed into tracksuit bottoms and his football top. He left the football in the corner of his room and tore the receipt up into tiny pieces and threw them into the bin. He placed the sports shop bag in the recycle bin at the edge of the estate and made his way down to the purpose built youth centre.

The building itself was the size of a medium community centre. Before Runi had renovated it, it had had an oppressive look to it, with boarded up windows. The inside windows had bars and the building was covered in graffiti all over the outside. Runi had done his best to make it look a bit more appealing. He'd got some youths to help him repaint the front door and put up Midnight Basketball posters. Runi and his team of volunteers had swept the floor, marked it out for basketball and repainted the walls a cream colour. Runi's budget from the council had included an amount to purchase basketball nets and he divided up the centre into two halves, each with basketball floor markings and each with their own nets. He'd purchased basketballs and whistles.

When the work was complete, Runi took a step back to admire it. "You done good," he said, beaming at the youths who had helped him, "now let's complete the look by putting up some basketball posters," and he handed them some adhesive strips and posters. The youths obliged. The room was complete. Everyone smiled.

"Midnight Basketball is the start of something new. I want you to join my team. I want you, to represent this place that we call our yard in our ends. I want a Holmville team and I want us to win the cup".

Runi Lancel was pitching his vision to the assembled assortment of youths standing before him in the youth centre. His talk was met by sneering, cynical glances, giggling and gog-eyed wonder. All those differing emotions coming at him and he knew and understood how each of them felt.

"Look," he continued pleadingly, "let's do something that we can be proud of. Let's get fit. Let's show other teams in the league that we can beat them and be the best. Let's have fun doing it. Let's give it a good go."

Tiny raised his hand. Runi nodded at him.

"You mean there's a league?" Tiny asked.

"Yeah. The Midnight Basketball League, and it's a good one. So we gotta be up to a top standard," replied Runi. "We'll play other teams. We'll win. I can see that you're nang, but you gotta commit to bein' a part of it. You gotta train. I want winners. We can be world-class. Yute who are serious, not time-wasters."

Runi pointed to a flipchart that he'd set up in the room. "If you want in, come up, write your name and contact number," he removed the lid from a marker pen, placed it against the flipchart and stepped back from the chart saying, "make your mark."

Lucinda raised her hand. Runi nodded at her.

"Can girls join too?"

"Wooooo" a mocking roar went up from the boys.

Runi raised his hand to silence the jeers. "Of course," Runi's voice became stern, "and girls joining *will* be respected."

Runi's face looked like thunder. The room was silent. No-one would cross him.

He walked to the back of the room and watched, as one by one, the young men and women walked over to the flipchart paper and wrote their name and numbers. Ten minutes later and the paper was full. A couple of people had walked out and ten stood with their arms folded, chewing gum and blowing bubbles. Runi walked over to them.

"If ya ain't joinin' ya can be on yas way." He pointed towards the door and the youths, who tried, and failed to outstare him, strode towards the door.

"This shit ain't nang, anyway!" one of them shouted as they slammed out. Deep down, no-one believed them and they didn't even believe it themselves.

"Don't chat to me!" Runi shouted after them.

The other dissenters left, feeling somewhat gutted.

"Right," said Runi to those that remained, "Let's see how many of you there are and we can divide up into teams and get started on a game. Those of you that aren't changed, get changed. Girls changing rooms to the left, boys to the right. No changing in the wrong changing rooms, or any funny business," Runi instructed to cries of "woooo."

"Karina, you won't be showing yer tits then!" laughed a guy called Jack. Everyone started to laugh. Runi shot him a look of serious disapproval.

"We want to have fun, but we're not going to be stupid!" he stated.

There was a buzz of excitement in the room. Even the most anti-social and problematic amongst those gathered there felt excited at the chance to prove themselves and feel a part of something, other than the gang culture lifestyle that many were sucked into.

"You have 10 minutes to get changed. Do it."

Runi walked over to the flipchart. He read the names. He smiled. Some of them had used nicknames and some were plain cheeky. The spelling was terrible in all cases.

10 minutes later and everyone was assembled.

"Ok," said Runi, taking hold of a basketball and bouncing it up and down twice. "I'm going to split you into two teams. No, you can't be with your mates. This is not about mates. This is about the team. I wanna see how good you are. Then we can work on techniques and improving and physique and fitness. It's about the team, stability and concentration. You need to come here, having eaten, so that you will be burning off the energy."

Jeb raised his hand. Runi nodded at him.

"Sir .."

"Runi!"

"Er, Runi, I haven't had any supper."

"'is mum works da late buses," laughed Marcus, acting out grinding motions. Everyone was giggling.

"Shut up!" yelled Jeb striding over to Marcus brandishing his fists.

"Whoa!" said Runi, stepping between them. He handed out two basketballs to each team and blew his whistle, "go and play" he said to them, and pointed at Marcus, who went off in the direction of one team.

"You, come with me," he said to Jeb, taking him aside to a corner of the room. The noise level was raised by the sound of basketballs bouncing on squeaky, plastic floor, and shouts of "pass to me", and trainers thumping and jumping on the ground.

"You gotta eat before you come here, or I can't select you. It's 'health and safety', bro. I'd get into trouble." Runi saw the hope drain from the eager young face in front of him.

"Do you have any food allergies?" he continued.

Jeb shook his head.

"Ok, look, I got a ham and cheese sandwich and a can of Coke in my bag. You can have that. Then you should sit out the first game to give the food time to digest."

"Cheers, Runi" said Jeb with genuine gratitude as he unwrapped the sandwich and bit huge chunks out of it, which he chewed and swallowed at speed. Runi walked away and back to the teams. The games were in full flow and everyone seemed to be enjoying themselves. He blew his whistle and clapped his hands to get their attention. The noisy sounds of running on the squeaky floor filled the poor acoustics of the hall, making quite a din, and the smell of adolescent sweat filled the room.

"You guys stink, we gotta open da windows," laughed Runi.

CHAPTER 6

Kieron O'Malley Mcdonnell had been 16 when he'd left home near Aston, Birmingham. His father had died when he was 3 and his mother had remarried a year later. His stepfather had sexually abused him from the age of 7. Always when his mother was out. He had been in pain. He had been in tears. He had been terrorised.

"You don't tell your mother anything. It's our little secret," his stepfather had warned him, menacingly.

Kieron lay wide awake with fear. The assaults were becoming a regular occurrence and Kieron was becoming withdrawn and introverted. He pondered telling his mother. They weren't particularly close but surely she loved him enough to accept that he wasn't lying? He decided he would pluck up the courage to tell her. Soon.

Later that week, on the school noticeboard, coincidentally he'd spotted a poster advertising a child abuse helpline. He pondered what to do. What if they were like his mother and might not believe him? What if it all got back to his stepfather?

He knew he'd get a beating from him. He just wanted to run away. He felt tears welling up inside of him. The bell rang to signal the end of the school day and the raucous sounds of children storming out of the building and the sounds of loud, boisterous chatter could be heard. At the end of the school day, Kieron never wanted to return home. He sighed deeply and glanced slyly up at the poster.

"Are you alright Kieron?" asked his maths teacher, Mr Foster, who was on his way to the staff room.

Kieron nodded.

"It's time to go home, the bell just rang, didn't you hear it?"

Kieron nodded.

"Run along then," commanded Mr Foster.

"I'll just go back to class and get my bag, sir," said Kieron.

"Hurry up then," replied Mr Foster and entered the staff room.

Kieron glanced left and right and tore the poster down from the noticeboard and stuffed it into his trouser pocket. He collected his bag from the classroom and headed to the park, where he would hang out for a couple of hours, until he knew his mother was home. He didn't want to go straight home and risk being on his own with his stepfather.

It was Saturday of that week when Kieron mustered enough courage to pick up the phone and dial the child abuse helpline number. His mum and stepfather had gone into town to the shops. He felt nervous as he slowly dialled the number, making sure that the home phone number was withheld.

"Hello" said the operator. She had a kindly voice. Kieron hesitated.

"Hello, what's your name? It's alright. You can tell me. You're safe talking to me" continued the operator.

Kieron replaced the receiver. He was in tears. Someone could be kind and caring and would listen to him. He felt comforted.

He decided that he would have to tell his mum the whole story.

When the discussion with his mother came about, Kieron's mother claimed not to have had a clue. She seemed to be in denial. It was obvious that she didn't believe a word of it.

"Don't dare repeat these lies again!" she shouted and stormed out of the kitchen.

On another occasion, when he'd just turned 16, he tried to tell her again and took her aside, tearfully pouring his heart out about it to her. It was the last straw for her. She seized him by the arm and threw him out of the house, accusing him of interfering in her happiness and making it all up. So, with a £10 note that he'd managed earlier in the day to steal from a jar of money saved up towards the household bills, he had boarded a coach from Birmingham to London. He'd arrived at Victoria coach station and remained in London ever since.

He was now 37. Life had not been kind and London had been even less kind. His arrival had heralded the start of hard drug use, paid for by working as a rent boy. He was now HIV-positive, due to a rich, older client insisting on not using a condom. Being ill, depressed and emotionally unstable, the drugs had taken hold of him and he was to all intents and purposes, psychotic, with disturbed thoughts and paranoid behaviour. All his dreams of making a living and starting a new life evaporated not long after he'd descended the steps of the coach he'd arrived on. He looked back on that day, in 1994, with sadness.

Spotting the arrival of people, usually newbies from outside of London, stepping down from the inter-city coaches at Victoria Station, was Vilis Vāczemnieks, a local pimp. Vilis was leaning against a lamppost across the road. He had shoulder-length greasy black hair, pock-marked skin and was missing several teeth. Years of drinking, brawling and chain-smoking had taken their toll on his looks and he looked older than his 32 years. He looked about 60. Vilis was wearing his long, leather coat and sucking on a toothpick when Kieron's coached pulled into the station. He visually sized up the young arrivals as they disembarked. His eyes darted back and forth until he had sourced the ones he thought would make the most money. A girl with a wide-eyed stare and beautiful skin texture had disembarked and was absorbing the dull, dank, Victoria coach station atmosphere with naive wonder. Vilis's eyes moved quickly. Behind her was a young man of about 17 with curly brown hair and of medium build. Vilis saw money. He saw potential.

"Come," he said in Latvian to the two cronies who worked with him and the three of them walked purposefully towards Kieron.

It was "the night". Jeb had waited until November, when it got dark earlier. Give the night time to settle, let the darkness terrorise further, he thought.

Naturally, his bloody mother was out driving the f-ing night shift. He had found out that Ashlee had been sleeping around with everyone and there was a rumour that someone had made her pregnant. He was very angry and agitated about that.

Lucinda had slipped him a note, under the desk in maths, telling him that Ashlee had come back from the abortion clinic.

Jeb was furious. Although he and Ashlee weren't an item, he still viewed her as his girl and was raging throughout most of the day. He'd been so angry that he'd punched the wall in the boy's toilets, causing the paintwork to crack. His fist was aching for most of the day. It was just the kind of rage that he was channelling for that night.

At home, he stood before the mirror dressed in black tracksuit bottoms, a black t-shirt and a black fleece. He placed the balaclava over his head and slipped the ski gloves on. His heart was beating fast. He started to sweat.

Shit, even *he* wouldn't like to meet himself on a dark night! He took the bread knife out of the kitchen drawer and posed with it in front of the mirror. He felt that he looked like a ninja. He looked evil, but it suited him. He practiced swiping the knife about in thin air and leaping and crouching. He was astonished at how athletic he was. The gym training and

Midnight Basketball practice sessions were obviously paying off. He felt like a warrior.

"Come here, bitch," he tried to make his voice drop an octave or two, to sound a bit older. "Do as I say, and you won't get hurt, bitch," he continued.

Then he stood up tall and looked admiringly at himself in the mirror, and nodded in satisfaction. He was ready.

"Maya, are you taking the car tonight? I do wish you would," said her mother.

"No, mum, parking's virtually impossible in Camden and you know the transport's quite good. I should be finished at about 10:30."

"Please, please phone or text me before you get on the tube. You know I worry."

"Yes, ok," Maya sighed, "I've got my front door keys, so you needn't wait up for me."

And with that, she breezed cheerily out of her home, never to return, as the dark fate that awaited her was about to change all their lives forever.

Kieron O'Malley McDonnell was bedding down for the night in the shop door way of a mobile phone shop on Camden High Street. It was a cold November night. His black woollen hat with Hull City on the front, a donation from the church shelter, was pulled firmly about his ears. He didn't follow Hull City. Aston Villa were his team but he didn't follow them either, as they reminded him of home and all the unpleasantness that he associated with it.

He unzipped his grubby sleeping bag and pulled it tightly around him. Although he felt it was late, he wasn't tired. He was a bit hungry. He watched the people going by, hoping someone might feel kindly enough to put some money into his New York Giants begging cap.

"There you go love," said a kindly, chubby lady placing £1 into his New York Giants cap and a polystyrene cup of tea down beside him. "You keep warm," she said as she walked away briskly. "This bloody government does nothing for the homeless. It's a total disgrace!" she added.

Kieron looked up. His wrinkly, grimy face smiled at her.

"Thanks love. God bless you." He blew her a kiss and grabbed the cup and sipped the warm tea. It was lovely. Just what he needed on this cold night. What could he buy with £1 though? He thought he'd manage to get a chocolate bar and a packet of crisps from the continental supermarket, probably without any change. They were open all hours, selling food from all different countries. Sometimes they donated him the odd bit of food. He'd tried Turkish delight last week, for the first time. It was alright but a bit chewy. Hummus had the texture of cement but the dates that they gave him over Ramadan were tasty and he loved the packet of Hungarian sausage meat salami that they'd given him last week, although it had made him quite thirsty.

Perhaps he'd be better off going to the local fast food joint and buying either a burger or fries. He wouldn't be able to afford both. Yes, he decided he'd buy a burger. It would be warm. He climbed out of his sleeping bag, rolled it up and picked it up with one hand, carefully holding onto the cup of tea. The pound was already in his pocket. His backpack was on his back. He made his way, cheerfully, towards the fast food emporium.

Sirens whizzed past him. The chill night air encompassed him. Hordes of young clubbers bounded down the street, their giggling chatter filling the air. Everyone seemed busy. Everyone had a purpose. No-one cared for anyone else. Shops were advertising Christmas items for sale.

He passed the coffee shop and glanced through the window at the warm, evocative scene. People clasping large mugs of various coffees, chatting amongst themselves about their lives. He sighed and put his head down. Such a world away from his own life. There was a very beautiful girl behind the counter. He didn't fancy women, but if he did … He looked up at her and smiled, lost in thoughts that if his life had turned out differently he might even be considered eligible enough to date such a woman!

At that moment, inside the coffee shop, Maya Fullbright looked up from the counter towards the window. She saw a grubby, unshaven tramp walking past. He had stopped and smiled at her through the window and she had visibly flinched.

At that moment, her colleague Agnieska looked up too. "You see," she said, "this is not perfect work, but we must be grateful, or we end up like that."

"Yes," said Maya, and she felt remorseful that she'd flinched, as she had seen the sad look in the tramp's eyes at her visual rebuttal. She made quick amends by smiling at him and giving him the "thumbs up" sign. In spite of this man's obvious sad situation, her sympathy was only for her own life and its current unsatisfactory career limitations. She still hadn't heard about her job application to RM3, even though she'd made the obligatory "follow-up" phone call. She was beginning to think she'd been unsuccessful and that her life would be an endless stream of never-ending coffee serving.

Kieron walked past the coffee shop. The girl had smiled back at him, and she had a

gorgeous smile, but he was hurt. It was like a knife had been pushed deep inside of him. The way she had flinched upon seeing him. These people. These clean-smelling folk. What did they know? Their life was as unreal to him as his was to them.

He entered the burger shop two doors down and felt everyone staring at him. He knew he looked and smelt bad, but undeterred he headed to the counter and ordered a cheeseburger for 75p. The counter server hurried to serve him, in order to facilitate his quick exit from the shop. Kieron's grubby fist uncurled and he held out the pound coin. "Thank you," the server said, and delicately, took the money from Kieron, trying not to touch it, or him.

"Shame I ain't quite got enough for chips," said Kieron in his grizzly voice.

The shop supervisor exchanged glances with the server and nodded, pointing towards the chips. The server filled a paper holder with chips, and placed the cheeseburger and chips into a takeaway bag.

"It's a cold night," said the supervisor as the server handed the bag across to Kieron.

Kieron snatched the bag, "God bless you, guvnor," he said as he made his way out of the store.

The other customers shifted, uncomfortably in their seats as Kieron passed them and exited the shop.

"Get the air freshener out," the supervisor instructed another member of staff and smiled reassuringly at the customers who were looking at him with stony expressions.

When Kieron returned to what he thought was his spot for the night, someone else was there.

A burly man, whom he didn't recognise, who'd constructed a bed out of cardboard and was trying to shelter from the harsh wind, had settled down in Kieron's spot.

"Oi, that's my spot!" shouted Kieron.

"Fuck off!" snarled the squatter, "I don't see anyone's name here." The doorway of the shop now smelt of urine and Kieron decided he'd prefer to move on and find somewhere else.

"Fuck off, go on! You woke me up!" repeated the burly man.

Kieron snarled, he wanted to bed down and eat his food and he wasn't in the mood for a fight.

"Yeah, you enjoy sleeping in that pool of piss, then!" shouted Kieron back.

He walked up the street in the direction of Mornington Crescent. Many of the shop doorways were taken up with other homeless folk.
Then he spotted a small shop that sold cameras. The doorway was narrow, but Kieron was thin, so he didn't mind.

He placed his possessions on the ground. The tea was now cold and the burger and chips were cooling, so he quickly laid out his sleeping bag and sat on it. He opened the bag of food and bit huge chunks out of the burger and grabbed handfuls of the chips. He relished every mouthful. It had been at least a day since he had last eaten.

CHAPTER 7

Maya Fullbright had finished her shift at the chain coffee shop. Her Polish co-workers were locking up.

"Ok, Maya, see you on Sunday night?" asked Pavel, as he put his coat on.

"Yeah, I guess so," replied Maya, smiling at him.

"Ok, bye Maya," said Agnieska as she stacked the last chair onto the last table and switched off the lights.

"Yes, bye" replied Maya who was halfway out the door and buttoning up her coat. She put her earphones into her ears and switched her MP3 player on, heading towards Camden tube station.

As he was taking the last bite of his burger Kieron looked up. Across the road he recognised the young lady from the coffee shop who had initially winced when he'd looked through the window. In that instance, he felt ashamed of who he was and looked down at the floor, hoping she wouldn't remember or notice him.

"She's gone. She didn't see me. Good," he mumbled to himself and drank the last drop of tea.

Maya Fullbright was in a hurry to get to the tube station. She had her earphones in her ears and was walking speedily along the high street. She glanced briefly across the road and thought she may have spotted the tramp that she'd winced at earlier. However, there were so many down-and-outs and rough sleepers in Camden that she couldn't be too sure and the lighting wasn't bright enough for proper identification. She concluded that it probably wasn't him.

The rough sleepers made her feel uncomfortable and she didn't enjoy the jovial shrieking of the young clubbers, who stumbled around in a drunken state, laughing and talking nonsense, on their way to the clubs in the Stables Market or the pubs that played live music on the high street.

Maya walked down Camden High Street towards the tube station and was greeted at the entrance with a big sign saying that it was closed.

Barbie Malozzi, a London underground worker, standing outside the tube station in a luminous, yellow safety jacket, explained to Maya that this branch of the Northern Line was closed due to a major signal fault.

"Damn," thought Maya, "damn it! I live too far to get a taxi home; it would cost a fortune." She didn't feel comfortable taking her purse out in public in this area but she knew that she didn't have enough money for a cab and she wasn't signed up to Uber. She couldn't be bothered to wait for a bus. She decided she'd walk to Euston station, where her options for other tube lines were more varied and she set off at a brisk pace. The cold wind whistled around her and she pulled her coat collar up tightly around her ears. Then she remembered that she'd promised to phone or text her mother, but by now it was nearly 11pm. She thought it would be a better idea to text, in case her parents had gone to bed early, as they sometimes did. She texted: "Hi mum, small problem with the tube, so walking to Euston. No big deal. See you in the morning. Love you both xx."

She put her earphones into her ears and switched on the MP3 function of her mobile. Pretty soon she was immersed in the sounds of her favourite tunes. So immersed that, as she approached the pavement near the front of the Holmville estate, she didn't notice the shadowy figure of Jeb, dressed in black, lurking in the bushes.

He had spotted her though, a brunette girl of petite build, big enough for him to overpower, wearing her coat pulled around her. She was the one. He broke into a sweat. As she approached the bushes that he was hiding in, he glanced in all directions and then lunged forward, holding the kitchen knife to her throat.

Maya lost her balance at the shock of being pounced on. Her earphones fell out of her ears as Jeb dragged her backwards, with his hand clasped firmly against her mouth. Her body was convulsed with fear. Her eyes were wide open.

"Shut up, bitch!" he mumbled at her, in a different tone than that of his real voice. He looked down at her, as she trembled, and, although he felt empowered, he also felt incomplete. This was not what it was all about. He should be feeling euphoric, but he wasn't. He felt angry with himself that he wasn't in the moment. He didn't even feel aroused. His right hand covered her mouth and his left hand ripped open her jeans and he grabbed at her knickers trying to force them down, but she clamped her knees together and her eyes widened with fear. She was struggling against him. It was not how he imagined it would be like.

He loosened his grip over her mouth, as they struggled. At that point, she let out a blood-curdling scream. A cry for help. A cry unlike any he'd ever heard.

CHAPTER 8

"Jebson Dunsmore, what have you done? What have you done?" Jeb was questioning himself, over and over as he ran and ran. He didn't know where he was running to.

"Be forensically aware" he told himself. "That's what they say on all the cop shows, innit. That's proper CSI-style!"

Then he put his hand into his pocket and felt the kitchen knife. "Shit". What would he do with this?" he wondered. He didn't want any souvenirs; that would be too weird. He'd taken the gloves off now. Panicking he placed the kitchen knife inside one of them and threw them into the canal. He was in a state of sheer panic with a heightened sense of awareness. He looked around the canal area from underneath his hoodie. He saw an old man walking a dog. Jeb ducked down and backed away. The dog looked up towards his direction. He must get away from the Holmville. The dog started growling. He was sure he was unseen and he turned and ran. "Avoid CCTV cameras" he told himself. There were CCTV cameras dotted about the canal towpath and he knew where they were located and how to avoid them.

He was on Camden High Street now. "Walk normally" he told himself, "Slow down." All around him life was continuing as if nothing had happened. He'd just nearly raped and killed a woman and no-one around him was aware of this fact at all. He felt disconnected from reality. He'd seen police cars speeding up towards the Holmville and an ambulance. What would he do now?

Jeb had very little money on him. He hadn't stolen the bitch's money. He wasn't a thief! He had no plan. He had his Oyster card. He'd get on a bus.

Jeb ran down Camden High Street towards the first bus stop that he could see. As he passed the old camera shop, he nearly kicked one of the down-and-outs who slept rough in the shop doorways and were teased mercilessly by the young clubbers that frequented the area.

"Oi, watch where you're fucking going!!" the tramp yelled, from beneath a torn and dirty sleeping bag.

Jeb was oblivious. He didn't take in the words that were yelled at him. He kept running. He knew he had to.

Arriving, slightly breathlessly at the bus stop, he stood under the watchful gaze of the poster of top footballer, Ati Adeofale, "the Nigerian wizard". Ati stood tall, serious and muscular with cool, short-cropped hairstyle, a square diamond stud in his left ear, wearing his team's football kit, with his lethal left foot resting on top of a football and gazing out across a packed stadium full of enthusiastic fans. Beside his other foot was the sports drink that he was advertising and the product's slogan, together with his signature. Jeb looked at the poster. The first bus that came along was the N29 to Enfield Town.

He boarded the bus without glancing at the driver, beeped his Oyster card, took a seat at the back of the lower deck and sat, numbly staring out of the window, without registering anything he was seeing. Two minutes later, his mobile beeped. A text message. From Ashlee. "Hey babes, are u up for it? Got some top grade shit to smoke. Meet at the towpath for a hook up?" He put his phone back into his hoodie pocket, ignoring the text. Reality was passing as a dream. Life was slow and disconnected right now. He looked up and thought he saw the bus driver notice him in the mirror. Jeb scowled, and pulled his hoodie closer over his eyes and returned to the window, where the world was unfolding outside like a slow-motion PlayStation game.

Yanos Kirygides, driver of the N29 bus to Enfield Town, pressed the button, closing the bus doors, indicated, checked his mirrors and pulled away from the kerb towards Holloway. He had noted the sullen youth in the black hoodie who had just boarded the bus and sat at the back of the downstairs seats. Something about him he didn't like. It wasn't just the fact that he'd smelt badly of body odour as he rushed past.

Yanos was middle aged and tattooed. He was a large man, not easily intimidated. He had once been good-looking, before middle age had crept up on him, wrinkling his face and giving his eyes a tired, hooded look. Due to his looks and his bulk he tended not to get too much trouble on his night bus. As soon as a fight would break out, he'd pull up sharply, step out of his cab and stand with folded arms blocking the front exit. He'd bellow that he wanted the trouble-makers off his bus and they would oblige, sometimes spitting at him or brandishing a knife or taking a drunken swing at him with their fists. It was lucky for him that he had been in the Cypriot army and was able to turn quickly enough into defensive positions. He had become a legend at his bus garage for once disarming a youth with a knife who had been stunned at the strength and speed of this "fat bastard". Yes, Yanos had seen all manner of low life on his bus.

"What had happened to London? Why were the people so angry all the time?" he wondered.

He sighed as he indicated, checked his mirrors and pulled into the next bus stop. He looked in his mirror at the hooded youth at the back. He was sprawled across 3 seats and staring listlessly out of the window. Didn't he have a home to go to?

Parents who loved him? Perhaps the N29 was taking him to his home? "No," Yanos reasoned, "probably on drugs," he decided, as a lady in a burqa, accompanied by two small children, carrying heavy shopping bags, beeped her Oyster card and went to take a seat near the front. A couple of Eastern European men, drinking from beer cans and reeking of alcohol were next to beep past him, jabbering on in an Eastern European language that he couldn't recognise and laughing loudly. Next came an old lady, struggling slowly up the steps. She smiled at him and thanked him for waiting for her, as she beeped her pensioner Oyster card and headed for a seat near the front. They were always thankful, the old people. Only polite people left. Yanos had a personal policy of letting the old people take their seat before pulling away. He knew some drivers weren't bothered but he had standards and prided himself on having them.

He closed the doors and checked in the mirror on the youth at the back. So far, the youth was behaving. No graffitiying, no shouting. Just listless staring. "Definitely on drugs," Yanos concluded as he again checked his mirrors, indicated and pulled the bus away into the night traffic and the direction of Holloway.

CHAPTER 9

Jeb was absorbed in his own world. He was living on adrenaline. All sounds felt like they were being heard from inside a vacuum. He wasn't absorbing any information or noticing his surroundings. He didn't think about anything. He couldn't keep replaying the events of earlier that night because it sickened him to the core. He disgusted himself.

The bus had pulled into a bus stop on Holloway Road. As though acting on autopilot, Jeb got up swiftly and headed for the exit. He strode off the bus and headed to the fried chicken shop.

"6 pieces, fries and a coke" he said, handing over £2.50.

"Eat in or takeaway?" asked the man behind the counter, in heavily Indian-accented English.

"What?" snapped Jeb at the man.

"Eat in or takeaway?" he repeated, enunciating more clearly. It depressed him how many people in England couldn't understand him, even though he had been a qualified electrical engineer, working for the government back in Delhi. Paaus Agarwalwas was indeed a very educated, proud man. Yet here he was, serving up junk food in a rundown part of London. Somewhere along the line, his career progression had most definitely gone awry, but times were tough and London was an uncaring city and he had to be grateful that he at least was bringing home the minimum wage.

"Eat in," replied Jeb, after glancing around the small shop and spotting an empty table.

"Enjoy your meal," said Paaus, handing Jeb a plastic tray with his items on.

Jeb frowned at him in response.

"Got any ketchup, mate?"

Paaus handed over a couple of sachets. They used to leave it decanted into plastic containers on the tables but the youths got silly, throwing it around, squirting it at each other and wastage couldn't be tolerated in these austere times, so his boss had struck a deal with a low value condiments company who supplied the shop with packets of sachets instead. He doubted the ketchup had ever seen a real tomato and as for the mayonnaise … Paaus sighed. He was a good cook, better than his wife, in fact, and in some small way, it upset him that the cheap food he served people was of the lowest quality.

Jeb sat down at a table in the darkest corner of the shop and unwrapped his food.

A television set on the wall was showing a 24-hour news channel. Jeb was pleased that none of the top stories had mentioned the murder that he'd committed just over an hour ago. Jeb felt calmer about that. Perhaps they hadn't even found the body yet. Jeb felt more relaxed. Perhaps he'd got away with it. He needed to think. He needed an alibi for when the police would find the body. He knew his mum was out at work that night. He sipped his coke and started to think in a more calculated way. The instinctive guilt that he had felt, coupled with "brain fog" was clearing.

June Dunsmore was out driving the late shift on a different route. She'd been delighted to have been accepted onto the bus driver's course that she'd seen advertised in the local paper, especially as she'd heard that the bus company had been on a recruitment drive in Romania. Now here she was - a bus driver, and at her age, too. Aged 33 and a bus driver! She felt proud, although she hated working the night shifts. No driver enjoyed them. The drunks and antisocial behaviour of the youths. Downright murderous some of them. No, if there was any trouble on her bus, she would not get involved. She had her son, Jeb, to think of. If people wanted to fight each other or scream abuse, best she could do would be to try and get the police attention by discreetly using her mobile phone. June didn't like trouble on her bus but London these days was full of scum and she wasn't gonna take the rap for their attitudes. Her duty of care was to her passengers, but her number one duty was to protect herself.

She had a photo of Jeb as a 2 year old behind her cab door, all toothless grin. What a lad. He'd been a great kid and she was proud of him. It had been tough raising him without his dad. June knew it wasn't easy growing up on the Holmville. Pressures, etc. She was working the extra shifts to be able to afford to get him the new trainers he wanted. Some Premiership footballer, Ati Adeofale, was promoting them. Top scorer in the league, rumoured to be wanted by Barcelona next season. A lethal left foot, or something. She didn't know, she didn't care for football. She couldn't tell one team from the next.

Jeb had finished his meal. He noisily slurped the remainder of his coke with a straw and scrunched up the paper that had contained the chips and the cardboard box that had contained the greasy, fried chicken pieces. He threw it defiantly onto the floor and felt delight as he saw the Indian man behind the counter look nervous. Jeb stood up and strutted purposefully to the door, his eyes meeting the Indian man's until he left the shop. Then he started to laugh. It was an outpouring of emotion. He laughed uncontrollably. Everything made him laugh. He saw a snogging couple as he passed the bus stop and could barely contain his laughter.

"You wanna give it to her up the arse, mate!" he laughed and watched as the couple huddled closer to each other and tried to ignore Jeb.

"You wanna fuck off out of our business!" the man snapped back.

Jeb didn't care. He felt happy now. He was confident that he wouldn't be caught. He was filled with bravado. What he wanted was a drink, but he didn't have his fake ID with him and so couldn't buy any in the shops or bars. He thought of Ashlee's text and her offer of marijuana and wondered if it was too late.

Taking the mobile out of his hoodie pocket he called her.

"Alright, Ash? How's my babe?"

"Your babe? What's up, where the fuck you been?" she shouted.

"Went to get someit to eat, innit," he replied, "Ash, we're cool right?"

She sighed, against her better judgement she replied, "Yeah. I suppose you be wanting some ganja?"

He smiled, "Hook up at the usual place?" he asked.

"Shit no!" she replied, "place is crawling with cops. They're scoping all over. There's been a murder. Some girl. It's bad, man. I mean, I feel sick. It coulda been me, like ..."

Jeb felt numb. After 5 minutes rooted to the spot, listening to Ashlee droning on about it, while he mentally tuned out, he composed himself. He took a deep breath, but his heart was beating so fast that he felt it vibrating throughout his body. His head was pounding too. Would this night never end?

"Listen, babes, meet me. Meet me here. I'm on Seven Sisters."

"Seven Sisters? What the fuck you doin' there? Wait - you with a woman?" she said, accusingly.

"Hell, no," he drawled, "no, no, no time for dat. We hooking up or what? 'Cos it sounds like we both need some puff. Come over to this ends and we can have some. There's this house, like, back of Holloway Road, like, which is empty, like. We can get into the garden, like. Meet me corner of Seven Sisters and Holloway Road and we'll walk there."

There was no direct tube line to there. "Ok, I'll get the bus." She hung up.

Jeb sighed. He slinked into a shop doorway and thought about getting his story straight. And he had to find a house, which would be easy to break into the garden of. All he wanted was to smoke weed and drift into oblivion and wake up in the morning with everything as it was before this night had ever happened. This night seemed to go on forever and his mind wouldn't let him relax.

At that moment, some youths in hoodies cycled past Jeb, eyeing him aggressively. Jeb felt a lump in his throat. He wasn't going to be a sitting target. He knew that he was out of his ends and could get beats for it, so he broke into a sprint down the Holloway Road and ran into the cinema.

Breathless on arrival, as he burst in through the front doors, he looked up at the security guard standing inside the entrance to the lobby.

"What film you going to see?" enquired the tall, well-built guard.

"Er, I don't mind," replied Jeb, "Let me check." He pretended to scan the posters on the wall but kept glancing outside.

The security guard noticed some youths outside, gesticulating and swearing through the glass.

Jeb was sweating profusely.

"We don't want no trouble here," said the guard, "so when that lot have gone, I want you to piss off! You understand?"

"Yeah," replied Jeb, "Yeah, yeah, that's cool."

"Good," replied the guard as he strode purposefully towards the glass doors.

"Go do one!" shouted a youth at the guard, making a one-finger sign at him. The youths cycled away laughing raucously.

The guard spun round at Jeb. "Now get out!" he ordered.

Jeb wandered over to the doors, peered left and right and slipped out into the darkness of the night.

CHAPTER 10

Yanos Kirygides sat motionless in his chair in the police interview room. He was wearing his bus driver's uniform as he had just finished his shift. His supervisor at Merchant Bus Company, John Stevenson, was sitting next to him. Yanos felt nervous. He knew he shouldn't be, but this was a high-profile murder case and he had been told by the police that he was a potential witness.

Detective Inspector Magnus entered the room carrying a file. He was accompanied by Sergeant Thomas Macauley. They sat opposite Yanos. Sergeant Macauley analysed Yanos's face. Yanos shifted uncomfortably in his seat.

Sensing the tension in the room, Detective Inspector Magnus moved to reassure Yanos that most people felt nervous in a police station but that Yanos was there as a potential witness, certainly wasn't under arrest or implicated in any way, and that he may have potential information that would be vital to the police in apprehending the suspect.

He offered Yanos a coffee. Yanos accepted, gratefully. Sergeant Macauley left the room to fetch the coffees and Detective Inspector Magnus opened his file. When Sergeant Macauley returned with the coffees and sat down again, Detective Inspector Magnus smiled and addressed Yanos.

"So, Mr Kirygides, on the night in question you were driving your bus. You were driving the N29. Please tell us what happened when the bus stopped in Camden."

"Well," said Yanos, taking a sip of his coffee, "I stopped on the High Street, as usual, and some nights it's busy and others it's not. Anyway, passengers got on and I noticed this youth in a dark hoodie."

Macauley and Magnus exchanged glances at this point.

"What made you notice him particularly?"

"Well, he was nervous. Somehow a bit shifty looking and, oh yes," said Yanos in a moment of recollection, "he smelled really bad."

"What do you mean?"

"What do I mean? Well, he had bad body odour. It was terrible. I was glad that he went quickly to his seat."

"I see," replied Detective Inspector Magus, "and was there anything else that you can remember about him?"

"Well, he sat quietly and seemed withdrawn, throughout the journey. He didn't do much. He didn't graffiti that I could see. He was just looking out the window. Quiet. It was somehow odd."

"Was this him?" asked Sergeant Macauley, taking an A4-sized CCTV shot of Jeb that was taken from the bus's camera situated alongside the driver's cab.

"We provided that" beamed John Stevenson, as Yanos looked shocked. "Police came to the bus company and asked us for all our CCTV footage from that journey."

Yanos took a large sip of the coffee. It tasted as plastic as the cup that it came in. Standard issue vending-machine coffee. Vile stuff. He preferred proper Greek or Turkish coffee, if he had a choice.

"Mr Kirygides, you look shocked," stated Detective Inspector Magnus.

"That's him!" cried Yanos in wide-eyed wonderment, jabbing at the photo with his fat forefinger and looking round at each of them in turn, "That's him!"

Magnus and Macauley exchanged knowing looks.

"We've been following his journey on CCTV on to your bus and beyond," Macauley explained.

"Where did you say he got off?"

"Oh yes," said Yanos, "he got off, I think it was somewhere on Holloway Road."

"Now this is very important, did he make or receive any phone calls or texts on his mobile during the time that he was on the bus?" asked Detective Inspector Magnus.

"To be honest, I wasn't watching him the whole time," shrugged Yanos, "maybe? I don't know for sure. I can't remember."

"It's ok," replied Magnus, "you're doing really well Mr Kirygides. This happened 9 months ago and we wouldn't expect you to remember every single detail. We have a CCTV shot of him on the bus looking at his mobile. We think he received a text shortly after getting on the bus."

"Maybe," repeated Yanos, "I honestly can't remember. Do you know who he is? Do you have a name for him?"

"I'm afraid we can't tell you that," replied Macauley, "all I can tell you is that we have a suspect in mind that fits this person's description. The suspect's mobile phone triangulation records show that he received a text while on your bus."

"I see," replied Yanos, intrigued. He glanced across at Stevenson, who sat proudly next to him.

"Mr Kirygides, you've been really helpful," said Magnus, extending a hand across the table and half-standing.

Yanos shook his hand.

"We'll be in touch if we need to follow anything up," Magnus continued, "but if, in the meantime, you remember anything which you think may be significant, here's my card." He removed his card from his top pocket and handed it over to Yanos.

Yanos and Stevenson stood up.

"Thank you, gentlemen, I'll show you out," said Macauley and he led them out of the room.

Magnus sat down again. He sighed deeply. So far, the police investigation had spent hours sifting through CCTV and taking statements from residents of the Holmville Estate, who had been home, or may have heard or seen something that evening.

Several people had named a "Jeb Dunsmore" as the person in the CCTV photo. A decision would soon be made about bringing him into the police station for questioning. Magnus and his team were building a psychological profile of the suspect.

Macauley re-entered the room.

"Bingo!" he said with a triumphant smile, "looks like we've got the bastard!"

CHAPTER 11

Simeon Skelton was bored. He sat opposite the young felon, and twirled his biro between his long, bony fingers. He twirled it to the left. He twirled it to the right. He marvelled at his dexterity. He was dying to flip the pen, but he had to look interested. His eyes glazed over though as he watched the youth before him, trotting out the same old excuses; "I never done nufink. It wasn't me." "I swear I wasn't anywhere near there", etc. Simeon hated Criminal work. It paid so little and the scum that he had to defend were the dregs of society, in his humble opinion.

Yet, humble was something Simeon wasn't. He was tall and lanky, standing 6"3, and very opinionated. He walked with a slight stoop to compensate for his height when walking with shorter people, and they were almost always shorter people. Aged 27, he had chiselled good looks; light brown hair and piercing blue eyes.

Simeon was seated next to his instructing solicitor, the brunette Emma McAdams. About 32 years old, he thought, and no wedding or engagement ring in sight. Emma's firm dealt in high street law and Emma was an accredited police visitation solicitor. From the corner of his eye, Simeon noticed that she had pert breasts, slightly visible beneath her crisp white shirt and formal suit. He felt as though slyly gazing at them was his small reward for having to endure the whining of this uncouth youth before them.

Simeon had been to Eton, where a fascination with History took hold of him. "Skeleton" was his nickname. He had a lanky frame and although he took part in all the sports that the school provided, academia was where he excelled. Studying came easy to him. He was naturally bright and didn't even have to apply himself that hard. He was a decent all-rounder, but he particularly loved History. History lessons at Eton meant actually travelling to the places you were learning about. They had learnt about the Ottoman Empire while travelling through Turkey. It gripped him with joy.

Simeon's thoroughly privileged background, his father, Jamieson Skelton was a banker, his mother, Charlotte was minor gentry, meant that he never lacked for anything material. Their house was a mansion in Warwickshire, tastefully decorated with expensive furniture and beautiful antiques from the Georgian and Victorian periods. They also owned a small apartment near Knightsbridge. Jamieson Skelton worked in merchant banking in the City during the week, returning to the family home for weekends.

Simeon was a top Eton student and went on to study Archaeology at Bristol, finishing the degree with First Class honours.

"Not quite bright enough for Oxbridge," his father would declare at dinner parties, to those who wondered why the eldest son hadn't followed his father to Oxford. "Doesn't take after his old man!" his father would laugh loudly and falsely, while inwardly sighing and feeling gutted that Simeon hadn't continued the tradition of celebrated ancestors who had walked the hallowed halls of Oxford or Cambridge. The boy was a disappointment. "Bristol, indeed!" he sighed. What the bloody hell was Bristol?! It almost sounded like an old polytechnic compared to Oxbridge and the grandeur that encompassed. Then he cheered up thinking about their other son, Charles, who had just completed his first year at Cambridge, studying PPE. That boy would go far! Simeon was the worry.

Upon completion of his degree, Simeon's father had called him into the drawing room.

"Close the door behind you, Simeon," he had instructed, softly. "Take a seat".

Simeon wondered why his father was treating him so formally.

"Father?" he ventured.

Jamieson, seated opposite the lad, let out a sigh and then declared, "There's no option, Simeon. You can't make a career out of Archaeology and I can't get you a job at the bank – hell, you didn't even enjoy that work placement I got for you. You were soon bored, twiddling your thumbs, looking out of the window". Jamieson's tone was irritated. Simeon looked down. He had done so well. He was pleased with himself. He'd even won the Archaeology prize for the final year. He felt low. He valued his father's judgements and he had displeased his father. He was a disappointment. How could he redeem himself, in his father's eyes?

"Father, I want to tell you something" he offered.

"Go on", encouraged Jamieson.

"Father, I've been accepted on a law conversion course and after that I'll do the BPTC," he breathed deeply, "so, what I'm trying to say is, I'm … I'm applying to the Bar."

Jamieson's mood lifted. He half smiled. "I see," he said, as the words took a short while to sink in.

"Yes, father," Simeon now had the validation he needed – the confidence to take this path, "I am going to become a barrister." His tone was decided, even a little defiant.

Jamieson was thoughtful. He gazed at the Cuban mahogany table in front of him.

"You know, the fact that you haven't gone to Oxbridge will go against you. The Bar is known to be elitist and has a tendency to favour Oxbridge graduates," he said seriously.

"I'm aware of that, father," replied Simeon, "but I thought I'd try anyway."

"Hmmm," muttered Jamieson, "well, I admire your spirit but it will be very hard for you because of that non-Oxbridge background, but you've been to a top Public school, and I will have a word with my good friend, Sir Patrick Lanbury, Q.C, to see if he could secure a placement for you at his Chambers. Yes, I could see him accommodating my request. Yes, yes," continued Jamieson, lost in his thoughts.

He stood up and walked towards the drinks cabinet. His son, a barrister, eh? He poured them both a glass of his finest single malt Talisker whisky, handed Simeon a glass and raised his glass, "To success!" he bellowed.

"Success!" cried Simeon, downing the warm contents of the glass in one go. The fiery liquid burnt his insides as he consumed it and his cheeks flushed. His instant reaction was to cough and blush. Jamieson laughed.

"I swear, I wasn't there. I never saw that woman in me life." The shrill tone of the youth, brought Simeon out of his daydream. He dropped the biro onto the table. Simeon's long legs were sprawled under the table and extended at an angle from the other side. Emma McAdams thought he was very fanciable and was in the midst of a saucy daydream about him. Simeon turned to her, as if for support, causing Emma to blush and abruptly snap out of her daydream.

"Ok." He said, "But, if you were there, if you *did* do it, it would be better to plead 'guilty' rather than go through the rigmarole of a trial." As soon as the word "rigmarole" left his mouth and he saw the youth frowning, he knew he'd made a bad choice of words. "I mean," he continued, "the hassle, the bother, the aggravation – the stress of a trial." The youth's expression changed as understanding spread across his face.

"Do you know what that means?" Simeon continued, while very much doubting the intelligence of this particular youth before him. The boy nodded.

"Don't you believe me?" the youth scowled. Simeon fidgeted with his tie. He felt uncomfortable in the youth's presence. There was something slightly sinister and unnerving about this particular boy.

"It doesn't matter what I believe," replied Simeon, "I am here to serve you. You are my client. If you wish to put up a 'not guilty' defence, then we'll plead 'not guilty' but it may prove difficult. There's CCTV of you near the crime scene, shortly after the crime occurred, and there may be DNA evidence. I haven't looked at the case file in great detail yet. However, mobile phone records place you in the area at the time of the crime and then in Holloway. Do you understand why I am saying we have to be careful to put the right plea in?" Simeon tried reasoning with the lad. Simeon felt that this one could be cunning enough to have committed the attempted rape and murder, but wondered if a jury would think so.

"Yeah," Jeb replied, "my mother couldn't live without me, if I went to jail. I'm the man of the family. I ain't got no dad. I don't know how she'd cope without me." He looked tearful.

Simeon wondered if the lad was talking about himself in reverse. He felt a little sad for the boy, but it was somewhat short of pity.

"Look," he cast his eyes down over his notes, "er, Jeb," he said, reminding himself of the client's name, "have a think about it, and we'll talk again shortly." He looked across at his instructing solicitor, Emma McAdams.

Emma had been lost in the gaze of this handsome, young barrister. So well-spoken too. She was somewhat reverential towards those who chose the Bar, instead of the dull paperwork of the solicitor. True, there were now "solicitor-advocates" who were granted certain audience in court but those she had met hadn't impressed her. The training wasn't quite of the same standard, or so it seemed to her. She wasn't one of them and had no intention of qualifying to become one.

Emma smiled and gestured to the cell guards to open the door. They all stood up and shook hands, the door clanked open and then shut as the solicitor and barrister walked out of the cells.

In the soundproofed holding area, outside the cells, Simeon retrieved his briefcase, his raincoat and his mobile phone, while Emma collected her handbag and jacket and switched her mobile phone back on. They passed through the security doors, a metal security arch, a bag search and then out into the fresh air of freedom. Emma took a deep breath. She always felt so relieved to be on the outside of a prison, or young offenders' institute.

"What do you make of our client?" she finally addressed Simeon, lighting up a cigarette, as they stood outside, at the top of the building's staircase.

"Oh, him?" Simeon replied. "Guilty, I think, without even fully reading the case."

"Hmmmm" replied Emma, dreamily. She extended the cigarette packet towards Simeon, but he shook his head. Then she made an offer to take Simeon out for a drink, on the pretext of discussing the case further. She didn't know why, she had just felt a surge of courage. This was partly brought on by the fact that she thought she had caught him glimpsing her breasts throughout the interview, and deduced that, perhaps, he fancied her too.

Simeon politely declined the offer. He knew how to be a gentleman and Emma didn't feel embarrassed or slighted by the rejection. For Simeon, the simple fact was that he had a girlfriend, Jemma Whitely-Dewitt, and she would no doubt be cooking him a fabulous and tasty meal back at the Clapham flat that they shared. Simeon felt flattered by Emma's invitation for a drink but he was not ready to betray Jemma, whose family were as wealthy as his. She worked as a fashion buyer for a top London department store. She'd been to Wellington College and then LSE and was extremely well-bred, and quite pretty. She understood the etiquette involved in hosting society dinner parties, and being on the social pages of Tatler magazine. It was a given that they would eventually marry and that their good breeding would produce choice offspring to continue their respective family lines and be junior replicas of themselves.

"See you in court then," Emma called after Simeon, who was halfway down the building's steps and heading towards the tube station. He raised his arm into a wave, without turning round to acknowledge her and moved swiftly through the rush-hour crowds.

Inside the cell a prison guard put his arm on Jeb's shoulder to lead him away.

"Fucking toff," spat Jeb as the door had closed on the other side of the room after Simeon and Emma departed.

"Oi!" said the guard, "no need for language like that," although he silently agreed with Jeb. The barrister seemed like a right wanker.

"Did you see how he looked down on me, that knobhead. What the fuck does he know about me, my life, my mum?"

"Come on," said the guard.

"Tosser!!!!!!!!!!!" shouted Jeb, sticking his middle finger up in the direction of the door, "If he comes to my estate he'll get proper shanked!"

"That's enough" said the guard in a louder voice, "Come on son" and he led Jeb back to his cell.

The word "son" got Jeb thinking. He'd never known his dad. He didn't know if his dad was alive or dead. He didn't know what his dad looked like. Or where he was from. What football team he supported. His favourite movie or PlayStation game. What would his dad think of him now? Here, in jail, for attempted rape and murder. He doubted his dad would be proud. Perhaps his dad had another family. Did his dad ever think about him? Did he even know that he'd got June Dunsmore pregnant, 15 years ago? He turned these thoughts over and over in his mind.

He supposed that his dad could be working for the prison service. Technically that guard could be his dad. "Nah," thought Jeb, "my dad would be fit not fat and balding like that old git" he mumbled under his breath as he heard his cell door slam shut and lock.

He climbed onto his bed. On the wall opposite was a large poster of the footballer Ati Adeofale, looking majestic and every bit worth his £6 million annual salary. Jeb took a deep breath and closed his eyes.

He imagined that he was Adeofale, on the pitch, in front of thousands of screaming fans, lining up that perfect penalty shot. And then, just as he was about to step up with his lethal left foot he visualised "her". The girl. Lying lifeless in his arms. Lifeless after he had tried to rape and subdue her. Oh God. What had he done? He felt disconnected from the event. Disconnected from the "him" that had committed these terrible deeds. Then his thoughts hardened. She deserved it. She deserved it simply by being there. What did she expect? She didn't expect to die. He hadn't actually meant to kill her. Just didn't know his own strength. Just gripped her neck a bit too tightly as he squeezed the life out of her. It was her fault, the stupid bitch, not his. And it was her fault he was in this young offenders' shithole!

He turned his thoughts back to the football pitch. He, as Adeofale, struck that penalty and it went straight into the net. Top right corner. Sweet. The keeper had dived the wrong way. And in his mind he heard the Match of the Day commentators praising the goal, the cheering of the crowd as "he" wheeled round in celebration and was mobbed by his team mates.

Jeb drifted into an uncomfortable sleep.

CHAPTER 12

Harriet Wokenham was a criminal barrister. She worked at Rosemont Chambers and had a reputation for being tough and winning cases. She was 48 years old and unmarried. She knew what people thought about that. She'd overheard the gossiping and allegations of lesbianism flying round the corridors and halls of the Inns of Court. Fellow barristers had slyly pointed and sneered behind her back but the simple truth was she was a career woman with no time for men. She deemed all men inadequate. She had lost her virginity, at the age of 17, to a boy that she'd met at the 6th form disco. It was the first time for both of them and was all over very quickly, in the car park of the disco. It was a disappointing, unsatisfactory encounter. The young lad, whose name she couldn't even remember, was highly-embarrassed at the speed by which it was over and was happy not to see her again. The feeling was mutual.

Harriet had shoulder length greying hair and brown eyes which were large and sunken. She was 5"5 and thin. She had once been engaged to a fellow barrister when they were both in their late 20's. They'd put a deposit down on a house and even drawn up wedding lists but then she had become panic-stricken at the thought of having children and giving up the Bar. It was not something she was ready for, or prepared to do.

Over the years Harriet had had other encounters with men, after she had broken off her engagement, but was very wary. No relationship had lasted longer than a couple of weeks. She simply didn't feel the need for a lover or a partner and had no time for the romantic side of life. It would mean her having to compromise and give of herself and her time and she wasn't prepared to do that. The law was her life and her life was her work. She equated it to living like a nun: Chambers was her convent and work was her vocation and chastity was now her way of life.

Harriet spent hours in the law library pouring over the Law Reports and keeping up-to-date with the latest judgements, attending dining in chambers and fraternising with fellow barristers at her Inn. She had even started providing podcasts for the annual Continuing Professional Development, or CPD, that solicitors and barristers were required to complete. She'd been approached by a company that made these podcasts and she had signed up to provide four per annum in two different areas of law. The areas that she chose were Tax Law and Employment Law, where she related and expounded her knowledge on the latest legal case law updates and developments. This was a tidy sideline which provided extra income, not that it was really needed. She was also considering starting a monthly blog, if she could fit it into her busy schedule. Many barristers had started to do this and these blogs were circulated online and via LinkedIn legal groups.

Harriet Wokenham's abrupt, no-nonsense outlook on life gave a sharp edge to her character, but juries tended to like that.

She liked juries. She could read them like a book. From the very first days of a case when they didn't know each other to a few days later when bonds had formed. Harriet Wokenham was an excellent barrister and knew how to present the evidence and get the jury on-side.

It was Monday morning and Harriet was sitting in her office reading "The Times" newspaper. Her door was ajar, which was how she liked it to be when she wasn't taking notes or reading up on cases. Her barrister's wig was on a wig-stand and her gown was hanging in the closet. She was wearing a dark suit and a lovely, but uncomfortable pair of kitten heel shoes. Although she didn't earn as much from criminal cases, she preferred them to civil cases. She liked the challenge of presenting a case to a jury. She loved the theatrical aspect of the courtroom.

Harriet had a sizeable income, which allowed her to live a wealthy lifestyle. As such, she had been able to purchase her detached house in Surrey outright. She owned a Jaguar XJ8 sports car. She maintained a good appearance by regularly having her nails manicured and her hair styled. Harriet liked to dress smartly but wasn't particularly interested in designer makes. As long as the clothing was functional and smart and fitted her slim frame, she was happy. She made sure that everyone in chambers received elegant and expensive Christmas gifts from her. After all, she could afford to be generous, with only herself to take care of.

The newspaper made for very depressing reading. The latest headlines were grim; terrorism, murder, the state of the economy. The headline story was that of the infamous gangster, Raydon Darnell, who had been shot dead by police in an Operation Trident raid on his flat on the Invicta Estate in south London. Crack cocaine and unused banknotes, with a street value of £3.5 million, had been discovered bagged up behind the counters of several milkshake bars which he'd owned and used as a cover for his money-laundering and drug smuggling activities. Harriet reached for her coffee cup, took a sip then pressed the intercom button on her telephone to ask her clerk, Richard Oweso, if there were any new cases for her this week. She buzzed the intercom but there was no response. Harriet hated inefficiency. Could Richard be late in today? He very rarely was.

Richard was 25 years old and worked as Harriet's law clerk. He was born in Nigeria and came to England as a small child. He still had the remnants of a Nigerian accent and spoke in a particular, soft and polite way. Considered a bright student he undertook a law degree at Queen Mary, University of London, but didn't know how much further he wanted to take his career afterwards. One day an opportunity arose to be a clerk to barristers at Rosemont Chambers. He applied and got the job, simple as that. He was always smartly dressed, in a variety of pinstripe suits, and was very, very efficient. He liked working for Harriet best of all the barristers in that chambers. She always came across as confident and determined. He aspired to be like her best values. He might one day take the bar exams but for the moment he was earning good money doing a job that he enjoyed.

Richard was wandering past Harriet's office daydreaming about the girl that he had slept with the night before. They had been drinking in a nightclub in the West End and ended up back at her place. Her body was superb. She was very flexible, he remembered as he reminisced about how they had done everything, many times, many ways that night. She was very keen to please him. He yawned. "A happy time." He smiled to himself.

"Richard!" Harriet's shrill tones brought him back to reality. Harriet had glimpsed Richard walking past her open office door. "Richard, anything from our instructing solicitors for me this morning?" asked Harriet.

"I'll just check" he replied and hurried off to find out.

Rosemont Chambers dealt with certain solicitors firms and were a contracted-out set of chambers that dealt with cases for the Criminal Prosecution Service (CPS). Ten minutes later Richard was knocking at Harriet's door. "There is a CPS case," Richard skim-read the notes, "a murder case. We will be for the Crown. Juvenile offender, possible attempted rape and murder, no previous form, apart from minor anti-social."

"Excellent!" cried Harriet triumphantly, "Hand me the case file. When are we due in court?"

Richard scanned the first page of the instructions "Thursday at ten, Wood Green Crown Court."

"Excellent that we'll be prosecuting and good that I'll have a few days to get my head round the case" replied Harriet with a broad smile as she took the file, "I shall have a read of this and prepare my arguments. Please see that I am not disturbed, Richard." She closed the door and moved over to her desk to pore over the case file, strip down the facts and make copious notes and legal arguments.

At her desk, in her office in her barrister's chambers, Harriet Wokenham was indeed making numerous notes. "Young man, Holmville Estate, single parent family, mother working, unknown father, no male role model, bleak future, blah, blah."

She chewed on her biro as she gazed out of the window across the green yard of Rosemont Chambers and lost herself in her thoughts.

"What chance at life on the Holmville?" It was constantly in the news for all the wrong reasons. There had been a terrible mugging there last year, when an old lady was left for dead, beaten black and blue. The previous year a father was found to have abused his baby. After a high-profile court case at the Old Bailey, the social workers and local authority were found to be at fault, the parents imprisoned, and the remaining children were taken into care.

Although she had not been involved in either of these court cases, she knew the barristers that were. They'd all shuddered at the thought of living on the Holmville. They were in awe at the inherent misery of those who had to tolerate living there.

What kind of people lived there and what upbringing, education and values did they have? And could she, as an educated, professional person, ever really understand? Could she ever really, truly empathise with these no-hopers? Could her ideals ever subsume her thoughts about living in a place like that? The latest news was that the council were looking into pulling it down and rehousing the families in lower level accommodation.

Harriet sighed, forced herself back to the reality of the here and now, and took a sip of her coffee, whilst continuing to make notes.

CHAPTER 13

June Dunsmore sat opposite Dr Shah in the surgery. She was not in good shape. He had prescribed her tranquillizers and a mild sleeping tablet. "Try not to take too many sleeping tablets. They can be addictive," he had warned her, in his kind and softly-spoken manner, as the prescription printed out and he handed it to her. She felt that he was genuinely sympathetic.

"Oh Dr Shah," she had said, "I … I'm not coping very well with all of this." Dr Shah looked across the table. She was a gibbering wreck. He sighed. He couldn't imagine what this lady was going through. His family were all scions of their community. His children were model students, although he suspected that his middle son sometimes smoked pot. Dr Shah had great sympathy for June Dunsmore. He knew that her life was a struggle and that her world had collapsed around her that one evening in November.

"It's like, I can't get no peace, Dr Shah," she continued, as he noted that she was anxiously biting her nails and wringing her hands.

"I'm seeing Jeb tomorrow," she continued, speaking fast, "at the young offender's institute. First visit since he was charged."

"Look," said Dr Shah, "See how you go on these items, and in a few weeks' time, if you feel no better, come back and see me again and we'll look at what we can do. OK?" he smiled kindly and she took this as her cue to leave. "I'm afraid, due to the new NHS initiatives, we can only see patients for 10 minutes at a time," he explained apologetically, as he sensed she would have liked to have chatted for longer.

She stood up, "Thank you, Dr Shah," she said as she headed for the exit, clutching the prescription in her hands.

Upon her exit, Dr Shah turned to his computer screen and typed up a few notes on June's record. He sighed very deeply. Poor woman, he thought. Life had not been kind to her.

As one of the doctors at the community practice, their patients were from the Holmville Estate and a few surrounding streets. He had known Jeb since he was a boy. Recently Dr Shah was hearing of Jeb, more and more.

One of the young ladies from the estate, Ashlee Jobling, had come into the practice to discuss a pregnancy termination, last November. She had named Jeb Dunsmore as the father of the child. Dr Shah tried not to delve too deeply into the private lives of the residents of the estate, or get too emotionally attached to them, but this was the second time a young lady had asked for a termination and named Jeb Dunsmore as the father. He didn't like the sound of it, but, as a doctor, he couldn't say anything to anyone. It certainly influenced his opinion of Jeb. "Next patient," he called into the surgery intercom.

CHAPTER 14

June stood in the holding area, before the entrance to the meeting room, where the prisoners met visitors. It was large, light and airy. There was a sanitised feel to it. June Dunsmore had completed all the security checks. She stood in line to enter the meeting room.

June felt very anxious. Dr Shah had explained that the tranquilisers that he'd prescribed for her may take some time to have an effect. June wished they would numb her senses. She wanted to be oblivious of everything. Why had this happened? Had she been a bad mother? What could she have done differently? Was it bad genes? These questions were recurring in her mind. She couldn't resolve them. She needed answers. She thought, briefly, of Jeb's father. It had been a one-off. She had rather liked him but he was just using her. He'd never returned her calls, and never wanted to see her again. She didn't even know what had happened to him. She didn't care. She mentally blocked him out of her thoughts.

Ever since the police had burst into their home, one evening, and manhandled Jeb out of the Holmville Estate, she hadn't been sleeping well.

"Suspect? In the attempted rape and murder of Maya Fullbright?" "No," she was horrified and remained rooted to the spot, "surely some mistake?" She had burst into floods of tears. She shook like a leaf and felt uncontrollable sadness. The rest of the evening had passed as a blur. The police station, the duty solicitor, being the "appropriate adult," etc. Sitting in on the interview and hearing the charge. She had been extremely tearful and Jeb had made it clear he didn't want his mother to be the "appropriate adult" with him. This rejection hurt her deeply. Could this be her son? Her lad. The boy she loved so much?

It was only earlier that evening that she had been wrapping Jeb's Christmas present.

"He'll love 'em. My son, they're for my son," she had told the disinterested young cashier who had served her at the local sports shop emporium.

"Yeah," the cashier replied, looking over June's shoulder. "Next customer, please," he called out, as she lifted the shopping bag filled with her purchase off of the shop counter and hurried towards the exit. One month of extra shifts had enabled her to buy these £120 trainers. "Creps" was what Jeb called them. Apparently this was the new hip word for trainers. She was dead chuffed. She had done it. Worked hard and saved up. One thing she wanted to impart to Jeb was that if you worked hard, you achieved. You could follow your dreams.

On the way home, she'd bought a fish and chip supper for them both from the local fish and chip shop. Her first evening home for weeks. "We'll have a nice evening in together. Supper, watch a bit of telly. One of those singing talent show contests. Or Big Brother, if Jeb insisted on it. Yeah. Nice," she thought, happily.

The wrapping paper from the pound shop was never a tough quality but Jeb's new trainers, shiny and boxed were now in gaudy, wrapping paper with brightly coloured pictures of Santa and Christmas trees. June smiled. She'd even bought him the football club Christmas card with Ati Adeofale on the front, posing with the team and embossed with the players' signatures. She wrote on the card, "*My darling Jeb, Merry Xmas, Love Mum xxx*". It wasn't original wording. She'd never been good with words, but it was from the heart. June had hidden the present and card in the bottom of her crammed wardrobe while Jeb showered and changed into casual clothing.

June dished up the fish and chip supper, onto chipped plates in their spartan kitchen. Jeb emerged into the kitchen and sat down.

"Vinegar on yer fish, Jeb?" she'd called across to him, while he took cutlery out of the drawer.

"Yeah," he replied.

"Ketchup?" she asked, holding the ketchup bottle towards him.

"Ta mum, I like having supper wiv you," said Jeb as he squeezed the ketchup out of the bottle and smothered his chips with it.

June smiled, "I know. First time in ages, innit. I'm sorry love, but I'm doing the extra shifts to make sure we 'ave a nice Christmas."

She smiled mysteriously but Jeb didn't notice. He thought he'd heard voices shouting in the corridor outside their flat. Then there was a persistent knocking on the door. "Police, open up. Open up!" The banging grew louder and more persistent. "Open up, we've got a warrant."

"What?" June was confused, "Police? What could they want?" June turned to Jeb but he had turned white as a sheet and remained frozen like a fly in aspic. At that point the police burst through the front door with a battering ram and spread out throughout the apartment. They stormed into the kitchen and all of June's hopes for a quiet life and peaceful, impending middle-age were shattered, possibly forever.

Deep inside the young offender's institute, the door to the meeting room was unlocked. "Forward, slowly please," cried the guard and all the visitors in the waiting area surged forward, towards a table to wait for their relative or friend on the other side.

On the offenders side of the door the guard at the front of the queuing offenders called out, "Ok" and signalled to the guard at the back that he was about to open the door with his entry card. He swiped it across the sensor and the door unlocked.

"In you go," said the first guard, as the prisoners shuffled past and into the waiting room, into a sea of expectant faces.

Jeb took a deep sigh. He was about to see his mum. He felt very uncomfortable. His eyes searched out those seated at the tables until he saw his mum. He almost didn't recognise her. She looked thinner, her eyes were red and had large bags underneath them and her hair looked lanky and unwashed.

"Mum?" he said as he sat down opposite her.

"Oh Jeb," she replied and burst into tears.

"Mum," he said, a little louder, "mum! For fuck's sake, don't cry. You're embarrassing me. I can't hug you. They won't let me touch you." As if to emphasise this point, a guard walked slowly past their table.

June whispered, "Jeb, I gotta ask you. Did you, did you k.kill, I mean did you do this? Did you try to rape and kill that girl, that Maya wotsits?"

"No mum," said Jeb deadpan, "no, I didn't. They got the wrong yute. Not me, nope!" He folded his arms defensively but he knew that he didn't sound convincing. Her face dropped in disappointment, as her voice became earnest and slightly higher than a whisper.

"I feel sick. Don't you lie to me Jebson Dunsmore. I ain't brought you up to be a liar, or a fucking thug. What the fuck's wrong with you? What have I done? I've been a bad mum. I know it. It's all my fault. They've got your computer. God knows why. What will they find on it? Jeb. Jeb, answer me!" June was rambling. She felt physically unwell and deeply afraid.

His mother rarely called him by his actual name – Jebson. He was stunned to see her so het up. Yet to see his mother weak and blubbering actually angered Jeb. His mind started racing. What would they find on his computer? Apparently the FBI had computer programmes that they sold to the Metropolitan Police which could find anything hidden deeply inside a computer's hard drive. Tiny had told them. His brother had heard of it when he'd done time.

There was nothing much on his computer, but if they could dig deep into his history and downloads they may find traces of his love for violent pornography. Stuff that was much nastier than the porn website that he and his mates used to get hot and bothered about. Women that were held down and raped, hard. Some of it looked real. Women tied up and abused, slapped around. They were powerless, those bitches. He loved to watch. He loved to watch the bitches subdued by real men. He wanted to be a real man. He'd love to try that. To prove he was a real, tough man that knew how to control these sluts. These whores that just wanted it. That would show these bitches how to be. The fucking sluts. He didn't know why, but sometimes his heart felt so dark and he felt so empty. He was a complete failure. Even this hadn't gone to plan.

Jeb glanced across the table. "Mum," his eyes burned into hers, "stop it! You're not helping."

He stood up from the table, pushing it roughly away from him. Everyone was staring at him.

"Sit down please," called out one of the guards in Jeb's direction, "there's 10 minutes left."

"I want to go now." Jeb spoke calmly. June was a blubbering wreck.

"Ok," said a guard and walked over to him. "Let's go," he said and led Jeb from the room.

Another guard came over, as if it was a real effort, and led June out of the room via the entry door.

June took a deep breath. "I'm fine," she said, when they offered her a plastic cup of water and some tissues. "I'm fine." She was gasping for breath. She wanted to get out of this place, and quickly. It was claustrophobic. Once outside she inhaled the fresh air deep into her lungs. She was shaking. She had suddenly recalled an incident from about 3 months ago.

She had been late night shopping at the local grocery store. She liked to make up sandwiches at home and take them into work for her lunch, as it was cheaper than spending money in the staff canteen. The grocery store was due to close at 10 pm and the only bread they had in stock was a solid, unsliced loaf.

It was discounted to 35p, as it was slightly stale, and June had bagged this bargain loaf and headed home.

She unlocked her front door and entered the flat, which was in darkness, apart from a light shining from under Jeb's bedroom door.

She quietly crept into the kitchen with the loaf of bread and opened the cutlery drawer. She couldn't find the bread knife. She searched around, and emptied out all the cutlery.

"That's odd," she thought, "cheap bread and I can't even make a cheese and pickle sandwich because there's no bleedin' bread knife!" She felt disappointed but was tired so she left the loaf on the table and went off to bed.

June had read about Maya's murder in the tabloids. A bread knife had apparently been found in the canal that ran alongside the Holmville Estate. Somehow this knife was part of the Maya Fullbright murder investigation. June remembered when first reading about the investigation that Maya had died from strangulation, so she thought nothing of it at the time.

Then she realised that their bread knife was missing. She couldn't piece it all together but deep down she had a sickening feeling about all this.

June decided to make an appointment to see Dr Shah the next morning to discuss, in greater detail, the antidepressants that he had briefly mentioned at her last appointment.

CHAPTER 15

Tom Rolandson was sitting at home around the tv with his wife, Sally, known as Sal. She was buxom and jovial. One of the reasons he loved her so much.

"Come here, Sal," he said, drawing her close to him on the sofa, and nuzzling her neck, causing her to giggle.

"Stop it, Tom, not now!" she giggled, in a non-convincing way.

"Grrrr," Tom teased her.

"Dinner'll be ready in a minute." She giggled, getting up from the sofa and moving towards the kitchen.

Sal always made top dinners. She was an amazing cook. A fabulous home-maker, and an all-round good person. Tom loved her so much. She'd borne him two great kids; Jody, 12 years old, and into fashion and girlie stuff and Chris, 10 years old, and into football and sport. They were good kids. They attended the local school and were doing well in all subjects.

They all lived in a semi-detached house on an ordinary suburban street in Bromley. It wasn't beautifully furnished but it was cosy enough for the four of them. Sal was a full-time housewife. She was extremely house proud, always tidying up after them all and their place was immaculately clean.

Tom worked as the stationmaster at his local rail station. The money was decent enough and he enjoyed his job, meeting people, and dealing with their travel problems. He had to wear a uniform to work which consisted of the rail company's v-neck sweater with logo on the pocket, a tie and navy trousers and shoes.

He was sitting on the sofa in his work clothes, untying his shoe laces, while Sal was in the kitchen, removing meat casserole, potatoes and dumplings from the oven and bringing them into the living room.

At the centre of their living room was a pine dining table with four, matching chairs around it. Everyone sat in the same place at mealtimes.

Pride of place in the room was the new 50 inch, full-HD TV.

"Jody, Chris, dinner's ready," Sal shouted up from the bottom of the hallway stairs.

The table was laid when the kids turned up and dutifully sat in their places. Sal brought the plates in and served dinner. Tom washed his hands and joined them at the table.

"Now, I hope everyone enjoys this. There's more if you want it," said Sal sitting down after serving everyone's food.

"Pass me the remote, love," said Tom to Jody, as she was the nearest to it. Jody pushed it across the table towards her dad.

Chris tucked into his food heartily. "It's lovely mum," he said with a smile.

Sal beamed with pride.

"Yeah, it's very tasty mum," said Jody.

Sal's smile grew broader. She lived for these compliments.

"Delicious, sweetheart," said Tom through a mouthful of food, as he swung round from his chair and pointed the remote at the tv.

The television sprang to life with the most horrible breaking news story. A boy of 15, Jeb Dunsmore, had been arrested for the attempted rape and murder of Maya Fullbright, a 23 year old coffee-shop worker. Jeb, a no-hoper character, lived alone with his mum, June Dunsmore, on the Holmville Estate in Camden, North London.

Tom dropped his fork onto his plate and his face turned white as a sheet.

"What is it, darling?" asked Sal, concerned that he wasn't enjoying his food. "Is it too flavoured?"

"Dad? Dad?" said Jody, concerned.

Chris chewed his food and looked earnestly into his father's face.

But Tom was in a trance. He felt sick to his stomach. He felt sick to the core.

Sixteen years ago he had dated a June Dunsmore, when he lived in Camden, North London. He was 19 and she was 18. She had confessed to him at the time that she was a virgin, and the thought had excited him. They had been on a couple of dates and he'd slept with her after an Oasis concert at Wembley. It was on the way home that he had had his wicked way with her in an alleyway near her mum's council house in Camden. She didn't have a clue what to do and he had been quite vigorous and, much to his horror, the condom they were using had split.

The way he saw it, she had been an easy lay, and he'd enjoyed taking her virginity. She'd been persuasive, though. It was not as though he had taken advantage of her.

"Tom, don't you fancy me?" she had goaded him, as they sat on the sofa at her parents' house, the week before.

"'course I do, June," he had replied as she let him touch her breasts. He cupped her shapely breasts in his hands and stared up into her face in wonder.

"Tom, don't you wanna go all the way?" she had persisted.

"You know I do," and he lay on top of her as they kissed and touched each other on her parents' sofa, with her parents sleeping upstairs.

"Well, come on then," she had continued, and reached for the zip of his jeans.

"No, no I can't June. Not here. Not with your parents upstairs. It wouldn't be right. They could hear us." He pulled his zip up.

"I suppose," she conceded, "but they never pop downstairs when they're in bed."

"Jesus, how many fellas have you brought back here, June?" he laughed.

"Not many. I haven't done it with anyone. You'd be the first."

He was quite shocked to hear this. He took a moment to compose his thoughts. So, she was a virgin and she was entrusting her virginity to him. She wanted him to be her first time. On the other hand, he'd slept with about 5 other girls. He probably wasn't a great lover but he felt very experienced compared to June. The other girls he'd slept with had been quite tarty and slept around with loads of blokes.

With June's revelation about her virginity revealed, the balance of their relationship appeared to change. He was now the one in charge, so to speak. He wasn't sure how comfortable that made him feel but sleeping with a virgin would be an interesting challenge and he was prepared to take it on.

"I've got tickets for the Oasis gig at Wembley Stadium, do you wanna come with me?" he asked, "it's next Thursday."

"Sure." she replied, ""Cos maybe, you're gonna be the one that saves me," she sang loudly at him and giggled.

"Shhhhhhh!" he said, gently placing his hand across her mouth, "Don't give up the day job!" They both rolled around on the sofa, laughing at her terrible singing voice.

The following week they'd gone to the concert.

On the way back, they'd got off the bus a couple of stops early. Tom knew an alleyway, off of the high street, where they wouldn't be disturbed.

June was breathless with anticipation. She thought Tom was dead handsome and she loved the way he dressed. They slipped into the darkness of the alleyway and had sex, leaning against the graffitied alleyway wall. It was hardly romantic but June thought it was thrilling and felt very daring indeed.

"The condom worked, didn't it?" she had asked him anxiously, afterwards, "because I feel a bit, you know…."

He was already pulling up his jeans and tucking his t-shirt in.

He had smiled weakly and unconvincingly at her in response. "Of course. You're feeling a bit, ya know, and condoms have

spermicide so there's no way anything could've gone wrong."
He tried to sound experienced. He felt a bit concerned, but
dismissed his own worries. "Condoms are very tough, anyway.
They're made of super tough rubber." He had tried to reassure
them both, so the chances of her falling pregnant must be low.

In Tom's mind she was a "tart", even though she hadn't ever
slept with anyone else, and he decided, at that moment, that
he wouldn't see her ever again. If he categorised her as a tart
it made it easier for him to let her down when she kept
phoning him, the following two weeks asking him if he'd like to
see her again. Tom just wasn't that keen on her and he
certainly didn't want to settle down, particularly if she *was* up
the duff. He wanted to put her out of his mind. She was too
needy. He just wanted to work.

He'd seen a job advertised in the local London-wide
newspaper for train drivers and that's what he wanted to be.
You had to be based in Kent though, so it would mean him
leaving the local area. He was mulling it over when his mobile

rang again. June's number came up yet again. He pressed the "end call" button and sighed deeply.

June appeared to take the hint and, after a month, she stopped phoning him. He quickly moved on to his next girlfriend, Suzy. Very soon he forgot all about June. He put her out of his mind and moved on with his life.

Tom had applied to, and was sent on, the driver training course, but unfortunately his reaction times weren't quick enough and so he flunked the course. However, the rail company noted his enthusiasm, and after a series of menial administrative jobs, he was eventually promoted to stationmaster at the local rail station.

During the course of the news report, a photo of Jeb flashed up on the screen.

Could Jeb be his son? He asked himself. Did he look like him?

Tom's mind was racing.

On reflection, he had treated June very badly. When he moved to Bromley he'd never thought twice about her. Could she have been pregnant? Why didn't she let him know? Perhaps she was trying with all those bloody phone calls to him that he'd ignored. Why didn't he pick up? Would he have cared? Probably not, he reasoned, although he may have made some maintenance payments to her. Obviously his name wasn't on this lad's birth certificate, as the newsreader called him Jeb Dunsmore, not Jeb Rolandson.

The shock of possibly being the father of a child he knew nothing about was compounded by the thought that this child stood accused of attempted rape and murder! Yet, perhaps he wasn't this lad's father. Perhaps he hadn't got June pregnant all those years ago and her next bloke was responsible. She was such a tart. Except. She wasn't. He knew that she wasn't a tart. He'd justified his poor treatment of her by convincing himself that she was. But, he couldn't be sure that her son was his. If the boy was his, he reasoned, this was his karma, for treating June badly. He'd never know. And yet, he had to live with this. He may have fathered a potential rapist and murderer. Should he tell Sal? What would he tell her? How could he tell his children that they may have a complete evil sod for a half-brother? Was evil in his genes? Perhaps his two other children would turn out to be bad as well. Perhaps this Jeb character was actually innocent and hadn't committed this awful crime. This Jeb had grown up without a dad, no doubt June had never married. He surmised that there must have been no stable paternal influence in this lad's life. In that respect, he, Tom Rolandson, bore some responsibility. Tom felt his heart lurch.

He looked at his children blankly. His heart was beating fast and he was starting to sweat. The cosy home life that he had built for them all was falling apart. It was built on a lie. He was not a good man. He had fathered a child from previous relationship who was evil incarnate. Yet, ironically, he was a good dad to his two legitimate children. Surely he owed this Jeb lad something, if he was his son? He should be there for him at this difficult time. Or should he? Questions, questions, all of which left him with a deep sense of unease.

"Darling, whatever is wrong?" asked Sal.

"Huh?" replied Tom, "er, I'm not very hungry. Sorry." He pushed his plate away and stared at the tablecloth.

"I know the news is bad, my love, but please try and eat a bit more," continued Sal, rather concerned.

The next news item was up – a corrupt MP embroiled in a financial scandal.

Tom instinctively stood up from the table and left the room, oblivious to the concerned looks on everyone's faces. "Sorry," he mumbled apologetically, as he left the room and his footsteps could be heard ascending the stairs.

"You eat up," Sal said to the children, "I'll go and see if dad wants some stomach medicine. He's probably got a tummy upset," she reasoned, as she hurried out of the room and after Tom upstairs. She felt more than concerned. She had never seen Tom react like this to an item on the news. And she knew that he was originally from Camden, north London. Did the story strike a chord somehow? Was he reminiscing about something?

"Let's watch The Simpsons," said Chris, grabbing the remote and changing channel.

"Yeah, ok", said Jody.

The news was very depressing.

Magda Jelovic, short with dark hair, green eyes, an aquiline nose and a large figure, was very excited. The pink envelope containing her call-up to jury service had arrived on the mat. She felt like a complete UK citizen now. "You see," she laughed across the table at her husband, "Stefan, you see!" She waved the envelope. "Wood Green Crown Court. Three weeks' time!" She laughed.

Stefan was very worried. "Magda, we must be careful. I am not happy about this."

The Jelovics had come to the UK in 2004 as part of the mass immigration from Poland when Poland gained entry into the European Union. Magda had been a qualified hairdresser in Poland. She now rented a small, local hair salon. Life had not been without struggle when they first came to the UK. Magda had started out as a cleaner in north London and then linked up with other Polish ex-pats and learnt the ropes about rental accommodation and establishing a business. As soon as she had saved up enough, she took out a lease on a small shop and turned it into "Magda's Hair Salon". She beamed with pride every time she drove past "her" shop.

Her husband, Stefan was the stereotypical Polish plumber. He had been greatly in demand, on arrival in the UK, and people liked his willing attitude to work and pleasant manner. Tall and lean, with very short-cropped brown hair and dark brown eyes, he set about working extra hours and taking on any work that he could. He had pride in his work. It reflected well on him, and his country of origin.

"He's so reliable" and, "He doesn't take tons of tea breaks" were remarks that Stefan was accustomed to hearing, as people that he worked for contrasted him with local, British workers. He sighed. It wasn't his fault that there were seemingly less jobs for British workers. Perhaps they should change their attitude. Work wasn't a God-given right. You had to be out there, giving something extra. He had saved and saved and now they were able to rent a two-bedroom flat in Islington, north London. It was quite run-down, but certainly above their expectations and to Stefan, it was their own personal paradise. When the recession fully lifts, he would think about speaking with the bank about trying to obtain a mortgage. In the meantime, there was work to be done and money to be earned.

He chewed his toast slowly and digested the implications of Magda doing jury service. He was afraid. He didn't like the idea at all. He just wanted them both to work hard and achieve a good standard of living. He didn't care about feeling like a citizen of the UK. He was Polish. They spoke Polish at home.

All their friends were Polish ex-pats. What did he care about being a citizen of this country? Obey the law, yes, but citizen? No. He was forever Polish. He never would think of himself as a UK citizen, as such. He and Magda always went back to Poland for their holidays to see their few relatives who were too elderly or infirm to join them in the UK. They watched satellite tv from Poland and his Leggia Warsaw scarf was proudly on display on the bedroom wall. No, they were Polish, end of. Life in London was good, but they would never integrate fully. Why would they want to? They had all that they needed.

"I said, how much is it if I want a return ticket to London and then onward to Manchester?" repeated the female, middle-aged, commuter in front of him.

Although Tom Rolandson was at work, his mind wasn't on his job.

Tom barely heard her. He was so wrapped up in his own worrying thoughts.

Last night he had confessed all to Sal. She had cradled his head comfortingly against her large breasts and stroked his hair, reassuringly and soothingly while he had sobbed like a child.

"What shall I do, Sal?" he asked, "that Maya was such a beautiful girl. Makes it all the more terrible."

Sal was deep in her own thoughts. She was horrified. Horrified to think that her children might have some genetic connection to a potential attempted rapist and murderer. She didn't know how to answer him, but she knew that she must remain calm and level-headed. This was the kind of information that tore families apart and she was grateful that Tom had confessed to her about what was bothering him. Nothing would tear her family apart. It was just perfect and no evil runt was going to spoil it for them all. Of course Tom had a past. She did too. He never knew that she'd once had an abortion. She wasn't ready for motherhood at the time, even though she was in a stable relationship with the man who had made her pregnant. Everyone had their skeletons.

Sal looked down at the man she was cradling. "We mustn't tell the children," she stated, "not yet. If it gets out, they'll be ruined. Their lives, their school, bullying. No," she reasoned, "they mustn't ever know."

Tom was sniffing. He absorbed what she was saying and he knew that it made sense.

"I mean," Sal continued, "It's not as if they're being deprived of a wonderful sibling, is it?"

"He might be innocent," protested Tom, "innocent until proven guilty. He's only 15, so how could he have overpowered a 23 year old woman?"

"That'll be for the jury to decide," replied Sal, matter-of-factly. Then she reasoned that she had better keep Tom on-side, so she added, "I can understand how you feel. It's a terrible situation to be in, and a huge shock for you, but your life now is here, with us. So, please, please try and put this into context, sweetheart."

This was not what Tom wanted to hear. How could Sal understand? How could she feel the deep sense of guilt and shame that he felt? He had to know the truth. He just had to. He couldn't feel complete again without knowing. He must go and see June and find out, once and for all, if the boy was his.

"Are you gonna sell me a ticket then, or what?" asked the disgruntled passenger shifting, impatiently from foot to foot.

"Yes," replied Tom, meekly, "£58.70, and at Charing Cross, get the Northern Line to Euston."

The disgruntled passenger entered their credit card pin number into the card machine and duly snatched the tickets from Tom's hand as she rushed towards the correct platform.

Tom made his mind up, on his next day off he'd venture up to Camden and see if he could find June.

It had been just that morning on his way into work that Tom had walked past a newspaper stand with front page headline pictures of Jeb and the words "Young Thug – the future of

Britain?" He shuddered. He thought Jeb had the same kind of eyes as him. The same eyes that the victim would have looked into as the life drained from her body. Jesus. He felt physically sick. Did he really want to draw himself into this web of nastiness, which in actual fact was none of his doing? Either way, the guilt he felt was immense.

CHAPTER 16

Vanessa McCreigh was making stir fry in the massive kitchen of her tastefully-furnished house. The girls were at university and had opted to stay up there this weekend to use the library for revision, as it was near to exam time.

Her husband, Dr Anthony McCreigh, walked into the kitchen.

"That smells good, darling," he said as he picked up a newspaper and placed his reading glasses on the end of his nose.

The headline story focussed on the sad murder case in Camden. He had issued the death certificate and he sighed as the memory of that night came back to him. He had also spent the rest of that night with his lover, Silvia. She had lifted his spirits no end after that terrible evening.

Dr McCreigh, put down the newspaper and reached inside his trouser pocket for his mobile.

It was on silent and had just vibrated, indicating a text message. His daughter, Amy had texted him. He smiled. "Daddy I love you. Studying hard xx"

He texted back, "Love you too, kitten xx" and placed the mobile on the kitchen table top as he headed for the cupboard where the cups and mugs were kept.

Totally oblivious to Vanessa's mood, he said, "That was a text from Amy to say that she's studying hard."

Vanessa ignored him and continued tossing the stir fry in the pan. She was smouldering with rage.

He assumed that, with the sound of the hissing heat from the pan, she hadn't heard him, or perhaps she expected more from her daughter's text and was annoyed that she hadn't been included in it, so he added, in a louder voice, "she sends her love to us both."

Vanessa added more soya sauce. Her heart was beating fast. Her mind was fixated on the dialogue that she had been mentally rehearsing all afternoon. She was ready to let fly with fury and spout it out.

Still no response. "Amy. That was Amy with a text." His voice was a lot louder.

Vanessa didn't respond. Her face was frosty and her whole body was close to trembling with rage.

Anthony didn't seem to notice.

"Shall I make you a coffee?" he asked her.

He reached inside the kitchen cupboard where they kept the cups and mugs and brought out two of the green Denby mugs, a wedding day gift that had lasted well, and placed them on the kitchen worktop.

Vanessa could contain herself no more. She turned the heat off the gas and spun round with a dark look of fury on her face.

As calmly as she could muster, although her voice was shaky, she said, "Who is Dr Brompton?"

Anthony was shocked. He had always expected some such question from Vanessa and had practised a variety of responses, but Vanessa's controlled and yet forceful demeanour had caught him right off guard.

"Dr Brompton is a work colleague," Anthony replied, thinking on his feet, while reaching for the coffee percolator and trying to act with calm nonchalance.

"Really?" said Vanessa, "That's interesting because when I called the surgery and asked for him they told me there's no doctor Brompton and that there's never been a locum doctor called Dr Brompton!"

Anthony McVeigh was stunned into silence. Calling up the surgery was the easiest thing to do. So easy, in fact, that he hadn't ever considered that she would.

He smiled calmly and reassuringly and asked, "So, what are you trying to say?"

"Are you having an affair with a doctor?"

"No," replied Anthony, immediately and seriously, "No, absolutely not." He tried to look earnest, but felt that he was exposed for the lying cheat that he was.

"Well, who *is* Dr Brompton. You spent last weekend 'doing research' with 'him', didn't you?" she shouted, before slamming down a tea towel and storming out.

"Vanessa, Vanessa" he called after her, "Come back here. Dr Brompton is the name of a medical colleague who is undertaking a research project on cervical cancer. He's not in general practice. He specialises in research. He doesn't come to the surgery. I'm merely helping, in some small way, to contribute some anonymous research statistics from my patients; patients who have consented to their data being released for the research. You have *totally* got the wrong end of the stick!" he shouted after her.

"Have I? Have I?" she countered from upstairs.

He ran up the thick shag pile carpet and into the en-suite bathroom, where Vanessa stood before him with make-up smudged down her face from her tears. She stared at him through narrowing, red puffy eyes, accusingly.

His heart sank. He had upset her. He moved towards her to embrace her.

"Don't you dare touch me!" she screamed, seizing a glass and throwing it at him.

He ducked as it whizzed past him and bounced off the bedroom carpet. She then burst into tears and fled into the spare room where she locked the door behind her. The sound of her sobbing was breaking his heart. She was the last person in the world that he would ever want to upset. He couldn't think of how he could convince her that he wasn't having an affair.

"Vanessa," he said, after he came up with a strategy, "Vanessa, I don't know why you are so jealous about a research project."

"I've never heard of it. You must think I'm stupid or something, but I'm not. When I went to stay with Sue and Oliver, and I told them about Dr Brompton, they said it sounded very suspect. How you were always going over there on days off, sometimes staying overnight. That you never introduced this 'Dr Brompton' or brought him round for a meal! You said you were on police duty that weekend. I wonder ..." her voice tailed off.

"I *was* on police duty that weekend. You know this high-profile murder case that's making headlines right now? That murder in Camden? Maya Fullbright? I was on-call for that. The poor girl, laying there, with a look of shock on her face, turning white – and she was wearing a coat. The same coat that our Amy has. It shook me up badly. I tell you, it made me shudder. The fear that she must have experienced in those last moments of her short life. It made me think. It made me realise that it could have, God forbid, been one of our girls. Maya Fullbright was only a bit older than them, after all. It made me realise more than ever that I *must* cherish what I have: You, and the girls. There is no-one else. I mean it, Vanessa, there is no-one else. How could there be? I love you."

He meant it as he said it, even though he knew that it wasn't strictly true.

Vanessa had stopped sobbing as she listened to him. She blew her nose. She had calmed down considerably and was rationally processing the information that he had just revealed. She knew that his job was stressful. She had no real proof that he *was* cheating on her. He knew that she was jealous. She did believe that he was on-call that weekend.

"What else did you do that weekend?" she asked him, seeking further solace in his answer.

He was thinking fast, on his feet. "I came home and watched a dvd. I had to switch off mentally, so, I watched an old Marx Brothers comedy. You know, 'A Night at the Opera' – our favourite one, remember? Good old black and white comedy. You can't beat them. Such a classic," he laughed as he sensed he was making a breakthrough.

She remained silent, on the other side of the door, so he continued, "On Sunday, I went for a long walk. I went to the pub for lunch and had a few pints then I came home to prepare for work on Monday. I was glad I wasn't called out again. I was so mentally drained."

"Do you love me?" she asked, "Would you ever leave me?" she sought his clarification.

"Never. I swear it," he replied. His heart sank, as he knew that this was true. There was too much at stake for him to ever leave her. He thought of Silvia fleetingly and sadly. He felt a pang in his heart because he truly loved Silva, but Vanessa was his life. The mother of his daughters. He couldn't walk out on her, or on them. He had to be the perfect husband and father. Some men did walk out, but he couldn't, or rather wouldn't. He sighed. The sigh of a man who felt trapped in his circumstances and too weak, or unwilling, to release himself from them.

She unlocked the door and hugged him. He held her tightly and stroked her hair. Inwardly he sighed, knowing he'd got away with it. Outwardly he kissed her softly and then more insistently, knowing that he would need to treat Vanessa very gently and be extra loving, to verify his innocence. Yet he was simultaneously irritated that he was living a lie. However, it was a compromise he had to make in order to continue the charade that he was a loving, faithful husband.

She pulled away from him abruptly and with her drying tears streaming her make-up-lined face further, she said, "What about the stir fry?"

"The stir fry can wait," he smiled calmly, as he led her towards the bedroom and closed the door behind them.

In the downstairs kitchen, Dr McCreigh's phone was silently and insistently buzzing as it vibrated across the kitchen table top with an incoming call. The words "Dr Brompton" flashed up on the screen.

CHAPTER 17

Kieron O'Malley Mcdonnell had bedded down for the afternoon in the doorway of a supermarket on Camden High Road. He knew that he had to stake a claim to his spot in the afternoon, or else someone else would claim it. The drugs he'd taken earlier on had had a psychotic effect on him and he was shaking. The world seemed strange. The High Street looked strange. Perhaps he wasn't even in Camden at all. Maybe he didn't even exist. Most days he wished that he didn't.

Over the years that he'd been living in London, Kieron had been in various hostels and on drug-detoxification programmes, none of which had helped, because he was too weak-willed to change his ways. Sexually, he was interested in men and had been beaten up by men in public toilets who had caught him glancing at their penises while they urinated. Although sometimes, certain men were more pleasant and disappeared with him into a cubicle to have sex with him.

He was scruffy and smelly and dishevelled. Earlier on that day, he'd been to the local soup kitchen, run by St Joseph's Church and eaten a hearty bowl of soup and a hunk of brown bread. The kindly volunteers always packed the homeless off with some bagged up supplies; toothpaste and a toothbrush, deodorant, soap, sometimes a clean top, a sandwich which he would eat for his tea, and a canned soft drink.

"How are you doing, Kieron?" asked the compassionate Father Mark, smiling, as he walked around the tables crammed to capacity with homeless people. "Never forget that Jesus loves you. Have faith in the Lord and surely you will be saved."

"I dunno about all that, Father," said Kieron, who found it very hard to trust people and form any meaningful friendships or relationships. He was gulping down his soup noisily.

"He died for our sins, you know," continued Father Mark, "so that we may have eternal life."

For some inexplicable reason, today Father Mark's words irritated him.

"My sins are too many Father; there's no heaven for me." Kieron was chewing hungrily on his piece of bread.

"We're all sinners, Kieron," continued Father Mark jovially, "but as it says in Corinthians 10:13, 'No temptation has overtaken you except what is common to us all. And God is faithful; he will not let you be tempted beyond what you can bear. But when you are tempted, he will also provide a way out so that you can endure it'."

Kieron drained his bowl of soup.

"Aye, Father, but I used to be a church-goer as a boy and I enjoyed my bible class. Does it not also say, in Corinthians 6:9, 'Or do you not know that wrongdoers will not inherit the kingdom of God? Do not be deceived: Neither the sexually immoral nor idolaters nor adulterers nor male prostitutes nor practicing homosexuals.' In which case, I, having been a male prostitute and a practicing homosexual, will not be going to heaven."

Kieron finished eating and stood up, stuffing his bag of free items into his backpack, he exited the hall, leaving Father Mark standing speechless. He had no instantaneous response to Kieron, or rebuttal from Scripture. His usual mantra that "God loves the sinner but hates the sin" seemed a lame response on this occasion and his face took on a look of shocked disappointment.

Outside the church community centre, Kieron saw a couple of old mates, Shaz who was female and decrepit-looking and stank of alcohol. It was impossible to tell her exact age. Her rotund face was covered in grime. Then there was Terry, who smelt terrible and had a similar lifestory to Kieron's. The three of them buddied along at the twice-weekly soup kitchen. Kieron presumed they were of similar age. None of them were native Londoners. Shaz was originally from Leeds and Terry from Devon. Being non-native Londoners was what bound them together in a kind of self-destructive friendship. They shared alcohol and drugs and swapped tales of bravado and paranoid outlooks on life.

"I made £10 last night," bragged Terry.

"Not smellin' like that yer didn't," laughed Shaz raucously.

"Fuck off, Shaz, I had a bath yesterday – at the homeless centre."

"His weekly bath," laughed Kieron, lighting up a nearly finished cigarette butt that he'd found on the ground.

"So," Terry continued, whispering in Kieron's ear, "I've got some crystal meth."

Shaz tried to listen as she crept nearer to them, but was drunk and toppled over, banging her knee.

"Ok," said Kieron and his bloodshot eyes lit up with joy.

"Give me a handjob and you could have some," Terry whispered in Kieron's ear.

"Let's go then," said Kieron and he walked off with Terry.

"I can't get off my fucking arse," laughed Shaz hysterically, but they ignored her and headed off to a secret place that they knew, at the back of the railway sidings in Kentish Town, where they wouldn't be disturbed and they could indulge their senses in relative privacy.

Back on Camden High Street, in the afternoon, Kieron felt particularly disorientated and paranoid. They were definitely after him. He didn't know who "they" were, but they were definitely after him.

"Why you after me?" he asked holding out his shabby woollen hat to a young lady walking past, in the hope that she'd put some change in it. However, she just sped up to get away from him.

"Got any money for a cup of tea, love?" he asked another young girl who walked by, ignoring him. "Well, fuck you then!" he shouted after her and burst into tears. The tears clouded his eyes and gave the world an almond hue. How amazing to live in a desert he suddenly thought. "No, good - you got the fucking Taliban," he reasoned and mumbled in his confused way, as a couple of young men walked past him. Actually, there were three of them, he thought. They were wearing Muslim clothing.

"Am I in Afghan?" he shouted towards them, but Ahmed, Abdul Mutal and Zohair just ignored him as they walked past him.

"That's what alcohol does to the filthy kuffar," said Abdul Mutal. The other two nodded. "Sad, really," said Zohair and upon seeing the disapproving looks from the other two, upon showing sympathy for the tramp, he added, "sad that he will never see Jannah as a Muslim, innit?"

"Yeah," said Ahmed with a disdainful look.

"Fuck me, how can Afghan have pubs?" Kieron wondered as the Rose and Crown pub opposite came into focus. His eyes were struggling to focus. Everything was hazy again.

"No surrender to the Taliban, or Al-Qaeda, or that other one, IS" he shouted. No-one heard him. No-one was nearby.

They must've gone. The government were sending people to spy on him. For sure.

He looked into his woollen hat. No money. Not even 10p. He cursed. He scratched his unshaven face. He was hallucinating for sure. That couldn't be his mum coming towards him with ice-cream, could it? Oh how she loved him. Just the two of them. Living in a nice, big house. Just the two of them. And he was a little boy again, playing on the swing in the garden on a bright, sunny day, while she made him delicious meals and looked after him, like a mum should. He smiled at the thought.

It was a woman and child with an ice-cream, but not his mum. They must have seen him smile though and thought he was smiling at them, as they were hurrying away and looked terrified.

Was his mum even still alive? Perhaps his evil stepfather had killed her. Sudden rage built up inside Kieron. Fiery rage. He stood up and roared and marched up and down. Then he suddenly stopped and sat back down, near his sleeping bag and backpack and his mind was empty and that was a good feeling.

"Excuse me," said the man now standing over him, putting a £1 coin into the woollen hat, "Am I heading the right way to the Holmville Estate?"

Kieron widened his bloodshot eyes to look into the face of the man in front of him. "Ha!" muttered Kieron, "fucking murder there. Whaaaa' you wanna' go tha' hellhole for?" and he pointed down the road, towards the estate.

"Cheers," said the man walking away quickly.

"Are you the government? Fuck the government. Stop fucking following me!" shouted Kieron, before he passed out on top of his grimy, sleeping bag.

It was 5 o'clock in the afternoon and Tom Rolandson lit a cigarette and stood opposite the Holmville Estate. It was an ugly structure, to be sure. Three tower blocks, with interlinked walkways on the first floor and steep stone steps up to the entrance square. Each block had a locked front door and a lift to take residents and their visitors up 18 floors to the top. Washing flapped in the wind from the balconies, alongside satellite dishes of varying shapes and sizes. The grey stone that it was built with dated it and added a miserable, bleak overtone to the structure. It was an architectural monstrosity built with a blissful, idealistic vision of social housing and neighbourly interaction that was no longer relevant in today's harsh and selfish world.

Tom had never known the name of it, or anyone who lived in it when he lived in Camden. Looking at it made him instantly miss his cosy semi in Bromley. How lucky he'd been to get out of London when he did. His home was ordinary, dull, suburbia as opposed to violent inner London with all its problems with immigration, social cohesion, gangs, drugs, pimps and tensions. Tom shuddered. I mean, just down the road a couple of blokes, dressed in all that Arabic gear, had tried to talk him into becoming a Muslim. He'd passed half a dozen East European shops. What was wrong with this country? Bloody hell. London was the capital of the UK and already he felt like he was a foreigner in his own country.

Where was June though? He knew what she looked like as her face had been in the newspapers. She hadn't aged badly at all. He, on the other hand, was beginning to show signs of impending middle-age, with a paunchy stomach and a thinning hairline. The press had portrayed a terrible picture of June as a mother, fliting from one unsuitable man to another and neglecting her wayward son in the process. He wondered if there was any truth in it.

Tom looked across the road and glimpsed an old lady pushing a happy shopper trolley up the steps of the Holmville Estate. She had difficulty lifting it up the steps. She was pulling it and pulling it, to no avail. He debated whether he should cross the road and help, as he had been brought up to be an old-school gentleman. Then he laughed to himself at the ludicrous notion that he was a gentleman, particularly in light of how he had treated June. His mood became deflated. He decided not to assist the lady. He would wait for June, instead. He sat down on the wall behind him. He didn't care how long June took. He thought the old lady may have noticed him, so he looked at his watch and then at the ground, hoping she would ignore his impoliteness.

Molly Mollson was struggling with her happy shopper trolley, filled to the brim with a week's worth of shopping from the super cheap supermarket. One of the wheels was loose and she hoped she wouldn't need to buy a new trolley. She'd noticed an impolite man opposite, smoking a cigarette and watching her struggling. He was dressed in a smart casual way and seemed middle-aged. She didn't recognise him as a local, but she was inwardly smarting at the fact that he made no attempt to cross the road to assist her, even though on several occasions it looked as though he was stepping forward to do so.

Finally, Runi Lancel, the local youth worker, appeared. "Are you alright, Mrs Molson?"

"Not really," she replied and he helped her lift the trolley up the steps.

"You know, if they made this block of flats nowadays, they'd have to build a slope to comply with disability regulations," he told her, as she disinterestedly unlocked her front door.

"Would you like to come in for a cuppa?" she asked, hoping he wouldn't, as her favourite tv soap programme was starting shortly.

"That's kind of you, thank you," he replied, not really wanting to, as he had work to do, but feeling she might be lonely and wanting a chat.

He'd been inside her flat several times before, to help her change a fuse on a plug and do a few odd jobs for her, and he remembered it for its chintzy furniture and twee statuettes of china cats and cherubs. Today he noticed that most of these items seemed to be boxed up. Large, sealed boxes filled the hallway and the living room.

"Sit yourself down," she instructed, as he squeezed past the boxes, while she disappeared into the kitchen to make the tea.

Five minutes later she reappeared carrying a tray with two cups of tea, sugar, spoons and Digestive biscuits.

"Do you like Digestives?" she asked, "They're my favourites, you see" she replied.

He smiled. "Thank you" he said, taking the cup of tea she was offering him.

"So," he said, "How have you been? Terrible business this murder, isn't it?"

"Oh, aye," she replied, "Did you know the youth? Was he one of yours?" she asked biting into her biscuit.

"Yes, I did know him. He was one of my Midnight Basketball squad. I can't really talk about him because I'm a witness for the defence," he replied.

"Oh, you're going to court? How exciting," she said with genuine interest and her eyes lit up.

"And before you ask me, I can't say if I think he's guilty" Runi continued.

Her face dropped. "Yes, but he *is* guilty. I heard it all from my bedroom window. I was terrified" she said.

Runi sat up straighter in his armchair. He wondered why she hadn't been called as a witness. Had she even been interviewed by the police?

"You heard it all?"

"Yes, that's why my niece in Ireland is coming over to take me away from here. There's been far too many murders and horrible things going on on this estate. They've found me a wee bungalow, near their village in County Wicklow, not far from my daughters and grandkids - and I can claim my pension over there."

"Ah, that's nice" said Runi, and he quickly downed his tea and replaced the cup on the saucer. He stood up to leave, as he sensed she was going to push him further with questions about Jeb, "Well, if I don't see you before you go, I wish you all the best for the future."

He smiled warmly at her.

"Thank you," she said, "And thanks for helping me in with the shopping, that was grand of you," she added, quickly closing and bolting the door after him and looking for the tv remote. She may catch the last ten minutes of her favourite programme if she hurried.

CHAPTER 18

June had been working extra shifts since the antidepressants had kicked in. She felt much brighter. More energetic. Much happier.

Work had been sympathetic to her situation, although she knew that behind her back her colleagues at the bus depot believed Jeb to be guilty. She didn't want to think about Jeb. He hadn't requested visits from her and she considered him the devil's spawn and felt increasingly detached from him. Whenever she thought of him, her heart sank and she felt an emptiness inside.

Recently she'd started seeing a fellow driver at the depot, Rob Dansley. He was a divorced man, with a grown up daughter who lived in Florence, Italy, and had a daughter of her own. Rob was muscular and tall, with brown hair, thinning at the sides, and dimples when he smiled. He had tattoos all over his back and upper arms. June was in lust with him, and he was in love with her. She had his total sympathy about Jeb.

After work today she was due to meet him for a meal in town.

She finished her shift, logged out of the depot, and rushed home.

As she walked through the archways of the Holmville, she sensed the other residents' eyes burning into her back, and whispering and muttering when she went past.

She approached her front door, with the faded graffitied word "Murderer" still visible, turned the key in her front door and sighed. She'd cleared Jeb's stuff away into his room and kept the door shut. She ventured in there once a week to clean it. In order to gather the strength to do so, she would turn up the radio and sing loudly. It helped her switch off mentally. The police had found Jeb's hidey hole under the bed, when they forensically searched his room. June's next door neighbour, Bill, was handy at DIY. She'd enlisted his help to nail down the floorboards and replace the small patch of carpet on top. In the spring she decided that she would totally redecorate the whole room. Make it fresh. Hope to put the bad memories of whatever had been hatched in that room, behind her. She had a deep, sinking feeling that Jeb *was* guilty of the crimes he stood accused of and she was tormented by it. She felt for that poor girl. She tried to stop thinking about it all because she was going round in circles with it in her mind and it was a mental torment that never resolved itself. She hoped that if Jeb did get off, he would go and live somewhere else.

June was in a happy mood tonight though. She showered and changed and quickly left the estate to make her way to the restaurant in town where she was meeting Rob.

"I'll have a bacon double cheeseburger with all the trimmings and fries," Rob told the waiter, who was writing down their order.

"And I'll have chicken caesar salad," said June, thinking that it sounded very exotic.

"What are you drinking?" asked the waiter.

"I'll have a beer," said Rob.

"I'll have a white wine spritzer," said June.

"White wine spritzer, eh?" laughed Rob, "Very continental."
They both laughed. Rob made her laugh so much. She loved
that. And she loved his brown eyes that were kind and sexy.

Rob took her hand across the table and held it. June smiled.
For the first time in her life she felt loved by a man. It was a
nice feeling. Unusual, but nice.

They made light-hearted conversation over the meal,
discussing Big Brother, other populist tv shows that they
enjoyed, and z-list celebrities who had had plastic surgery or
married and divorced.

"Wanna come back to mine for a nightcap?" asked June with a
wink.

Rob smiled, "'Course I do!" He settled the bill and they left the
restaurant.

They stepped out into Leicester Square. The West End was
bustling with people and Rob held June tightly and guided her

through the crowds. "Are we going by bus?" asked Rob jokingly and they both collapsed into fits of giggles.

Upon arrival in Camden, Rob parked his car in a resident permit holders' space, two minutes down the road from the entrance to the Holmville.

"You'll be alright here till the morning," June reassured him and they walked arm-in-arm towards the Holmville.

It was dark and chilly. Tom had been waiting across the road for 3 hours. His mobile rang. It was Sal. He let it go to voicemail.

"Hi, honey, it's me, please give me a ring and let me know what time you'll be back for dinner. I love you." The message ended. Just as he was pressing the delete button, he noticed June, with a bloke draped over her, walking down the road. Damn! He'd wanted to speak to her on her own. He turned around and lit a cigarette, so that he wouldn't look suspicious, but it was too late. He'd been spotted.

"Who's that?" asked Rob.

"No idea, let's get in quick. You get all sorts of randomers hanging around 'ere at night," replied June.

"June?" the man called out. "June Dunsmore, is that you?"

Rob looked back angrily and gestured with a one-finger sign. "Fuck off! She's not talking to the press."

"I ain't the press. I think I might be. I might be Jeb's father," came the reply.

June dropped her house keys in shock, and spun round to look at Tom. It was dark, she'd drunk a couple of white wine spritzers and she squinted across the road but it was hard to visualise Tom too clearly.

"Well, if you are, you're 15 years too late!" she screamed back, before turning to Rob, who had picked up her keys. "Let's go inside" she said to him and they disappeared through the glass-fronted, heavily fortified entrance doors to the Holmville.

Tom sprinted across the road but the Holmville doors were firmly shut and he arrived there just in time to see June, and the man she was with, disappearing into the lift.

"Damn!" thought Tom. Obviously she didn't want to speak to him. Perhaps it was because of the chap she was with. He didn't seem too lovely. Tom felt that this was useless and resigned himself to returning home to Bromley without the answers that he so desperately needed. His mind was racing about how to explain to his family about where he had been and why he had been out for so long.

He was so preoccupied with his thoughts that he was unaware of some youths in hoodies watching him. When he looked up, they were drawing menacingly closer to him and he felt afraid. He knew that in London these days, anyone could be knifed for "looking at someone the wrong way" – whatever that meant. People were on short fuses and ready to kick off at the least provocation. Many young people were tooled up with knives.

"Dat's a nice watch you got there, bro," said one of the youths, nodding intimidatingly at Tom, "I tink you should hand it over and we let you go peacefully, know what I mean?"

Tom backed away slowly and on turning ran as fast as he could. He heard the click of a switchblade being flicked open. A cry of "Get 'im!" went up and the youths broke into a sprint behind Tom, as he headed for Mornington Crescent tube station. The ringleader, who was on a bicycle peddled frantically alongside them, picking up speed while goading them on.

Who were these youths? Were they friends of Jeb's, or were they some other youths? Either way, he wasn't going to hang around to find out. He tore into Mornington Crescent tube station with the last fibre of his breath and frantically jabbed at the lift buttons.

"Come on, come on," he yelled at the lifts in a panic. Another commuter, a slim woman with mousey brown hair, about 30 years old, stared at him, wondering what was going on. There was a cacophony outside from the youths as they approached the tube station and lots of shouting, swearing and jeering. It was an unnerving, collective sound that shattered any mental tranquillity.

The lift doors opened. The other commuter stepped uneasily into the lift with Tom and the doors closed. Tom tried to smile politely, to put the lady at her ease, but sensed that he may have made her feel even more uncomfortable, as she took a step away from him and huddled against the wall of the lift, looking up into the small, CCTV camera, hoping to be noticed in the event of a crime, or someone live monitoring the lift.

Tom didn't care. He breathed a visible sigh of relief. Should the youths decided to take the stairs, he'd be down on the platform and onto a train before they'd even gone down ten steps.

The youths reached the tube station two minutes after him. One of them pointed up at the CCTV camera at the ticket hall entrance, and as they saw no sign of Tom, they decided not to pursue him into the tube station and ran off.

Tom was still out of breath and wheezing and gasping when the tube train pulled up on the platform. Too many of Sal's delicious home-cooked meals and he knew he was overweight and under fit. The Northern Line tube delivered him safely to Charing Cross Station, where he used his concessionary staff travel pass to take the train back to Bromley. During the journey, Tom reflected on how terrified he'd felt. He wouldn't be returning to Camden, if he could help it. The area had unquestionably gone downhill since he lived there. It put into context the life that Jeb must have lived and who he might have been mixing with. In his mind, Jeb must therefore be guilty of the crime and he must put Jeb out of his mind, like Sal had said, and move on with the life he was now leading with his family.

And yet, he just had to know.

CHAPTER 19

Tessa and Harold Fullbright were sitting with the Police Family Liaison Officer who had been assigned to them at the beginning of the case. The trial was coming up soon. The months of waiting had been agony but they had been assured by their solicitor that the police had got their man and that a jury would definitely convict him.

Tessa and Harold's world had been wrenched apart by the news that their one and only daughter's life had been taken and that she had endured the indignity of being sexually assaulted and murdered by some young hoodlum in the process.

Their living room was still full of sympathy cards and messages.

Maya's bedroom upstairs remained untouched, as a shrine to her.

Some evenings Tessa would go in there and lie on Maya's bed, just to feel close to her. She would hold a t-shirt that still had a remnant of Maya's scent, close to her and she would sob uncontrollably. Sometimes she "talked" to Maya, telling her how their day had been.

"You've no idea how impotent I feel as a father," said Harold, "that I couldn't protect my little girl." Tessa burst into floods of tears. The constant weeping had caused the thin skin under her eyes, and down her chin to form channels on her face. She looked gaunt.

Neither of them were eating well.

Harold and Tessa were traditional and orthodox in their thinking. As such, they'd turned down numerous offers of grief counselling, thinking it "New Age" and "claptrap". They preferred to grieve alone, together, away from professional eyes. They were private people and it was bad enough having to have the Police Liaison Officer visiting them on a daily basis.

"I had a dream last night, that Maya was calling out to me, and I tried to reach her and then, darkness and I woke up," said Tessa.

They'd both had vivid dreams.

"I hope she didn't suffer too much," added Tessa and then burst into floods of tears.

The constant cycle of emotions: anger, tears, rage, despair and hopelessness overwhelmed them both and they couldn't see an end to it all. They knew that they would never feel complete happiness again.

"Sometimes, I wish I were dead, so that I could see her again," said Harold, sighing heavily.

"I suppose that's one advantage to being older parents," said Tessa. They both semi-smiled.

"I know it sounds like a cliché, but time really *is* a great healer," said the Police Liaison Officer.

They looked at her. A young girl of 20-something; only slightly older than their beloved Maya. What experience did she have of the world, or of life in general? Was she married? They didn't think so, as she didn't wear a wedding ring. Did she have children? It was a possibility in today's immoral world.

Tessa opened her mouth to make a retort, but Harold raised his hand in a gesture of silence and the two of them sat in their living room, looking at the carpet in stony silence.

Sensing she may have said the wrong thing, the Police Liaison Officer, piped up, "I'll make us all a cup of tea" and she stood up and went into the kitchen, relieved to leave the heavy atmosphere, albeit only temporarily.

This scenario had been playing out daily, for months, ever since the youth from that dreadful estate had been charged with Maya's murder.

The irony of the whole thing was that Maya had got the job that she had applied for. The letter offering her a contract with RM3 Recruitment had landed on the doormat two days after her death. The post had been slow. The letter reached the house two days later than expected. Maya could've handed her notice in and left the café two days before she was murdered. She might still be alive.

"Even after her death, she makes us proud," sobbed Tessa uncontrollably, as she clung to the letter, after opening it. Harold, who had been brought up to supress emotion, didn't know how to comfort her. He held her in his arms and silently grieved inwardly for his beautiful, little girl.

Every day they visited her graveyard in the local church and laid fresh flowers. It was therapeutic to "talk" to her. They discussed trivial, jovial matters, never mentioning the upcoming trial or anything related to it.

The trial was approaching. The trial date had been set for October, nearly a year since Maya's murder.

They had tried many times to think up a "witness impact statement" that would be read out at the end of the trial, if the defendant was found guilty. It never got any easier to explain how their lives had been torn apart forever by the crazed actions of an evil person. How angry they were that Maya hadn't handed her notice in had her job offer letter been received on the correct day. How sad they then felt that it might have been someone else's daughter who would've then been in the wrong place at the wrong time and confronted by Jeb. The bad luck they felt they had that the tube line had suffered a major signal fault on that fateful night. It seemed as if the heavens had conspired against them to rob them of their only child.

They took some small comfort in the fact that they were told that Maya had fought back and that she had protected her dignity by preventing herself from being raped. Yet, it was small comfort. Their daughter's young life, so full of potential, had been snuffed out. It made no sense at all. Maya was a good girl, waiting for a lucky break career-wise, and she would have been a success, of that her parents were sure. She would have gone on to marry and have children. They mourned the loss of Maya and her future and any grandchildren that they might have known. As her future was over, so, in effect, was theirs.

"Oh, he'll be found guilty alright," said the Police Liaison Officer, confidently "there's CCTV footage of him, DNA evidence, witnesses," although she didn't tell the Fullbrights that one potential witness was now living in Ireland and some old tramp, who the defendant had been seen kicking on CCTV, whilst making his getaway, may be so unreliable a witness that he may not even be called to take the stand. She thought it would be therapeutic for the Fullbrights to put their witness impact statement together. Their solicitor, Jonathan Lisington, kept badgering her to get the Fullbrights to make the statement.

"They just won't do it. Sorry," she told Lisington. "It's alright," said Lisington, "Sometimes it takes the trial to kick into gear the emotion and words that can motivate a bereaved family."

It was as dull a Sunday as Sunday could ever be. The overcast London skies and the continuous rain were reflected in the windows of Silvia's apartment. Dr Anthony McCreigh had decided to tell Silvia about the close encounter he'd had with Vanessa. Silvia had acted coolly but was quite jealous and angry that he appeared to be favouring Vanessa over her. She had sat stony-faced and unemotional as he had banged on about "Vanessa" and having to save his marriage. "The issuing of the death certificate for Maya Fullbright really brought it all home to me," he continued. Silvia despised weakness in a man. Anthony's attitude really jarred on her.

"I'd better go now," he said, "but I'll just use the bathroom first, ok?" He smiled, but his smile couldn't warm her mood or soften her heart.

As soon as he stood up and left the room for the bathroom, Silvia rushed into the bedroom and started rummaging around in her underwear drawer. In a moment of spite, she found a pair of her silky knickers and planted them in the inside pocket of Anthony's jacket. She knew that Vanessa would take this jacket to the dry cleaners for him. She felt triumphant. Her jealous, but silent rage was quenched. She was satisfied.

Dr McCreigh returned from the bathroom and put his jacket on.

"Goodbye, my love," he said, as he planted a kiss on Silvia's lips.

"Yes, goodbye," she replied, somewhat coolly. He closed the apartment door behind him and she rushed into the master bedroom and drew back the curtains to watch him walk to his car. She looked down upon him striding towards his car in the pouring rain and felt justified in her actions. She had forced his hand by doing this. He would have to choose between them now. She realised in that moment that she loved this man deeply. She didn't want to lose him. She felt warm inside when she thought about him and she smiled and waved as she watched him drive off in the direction of his house. Silvia was lost in her thoughts. She walked over to look at a framed photo of the two of them that she kept on the bedside table. They were walking in the street when they took that "selfie." It was after they'd seen a show in the West End and they were both laughing and carefree. Silvia smiled at the memory.

However, Silvia was a pragmatic person. She knew Anthony well enough to know that, due to his circumstances, he would always choose Vanessa over her. He had to. He was an excellent doctor, a respected member of the community and an adoring father. She felt wretched that she couldn't be with him the whole time but she realised that she had quite a good compromise situation.

In that instance, Silvia suddenly regretted planting the underwear, but knew it might be too late. She fetched her handbag and reached for her mobile phone.

Dr McCreigh turned the key in the door of his house, closed the door behind him and entered the living room.

"Hello darling," said Vanessa as she approached him and kissed him on the lips.

"Hello my love," he replied, smiling at her, as he took his jacket off.

"Here let me take that," said Vanessa, "I'll take it to the dry cleaners tomorrow morning."

"Thank you. I may have some other stuff to go," Anthony called after her, as he sat on the sofa and reached for the newspaper.

Vanessa carried the jacket to the utility room, adjoining the kitchen.

As soon as she'd walked away, Dr McCreigh looked at the text message that he had not been able to look at whilst driving. It was from "Dr Brompton." It read "Don't give her the jacket! I put a surprise underwear in the inside pocket."

Anthony frowned, digesting this information, and his face darkened. Vanessa re-entered the room at that moment. Her demeanour had noticeably cooled.

CHAPTER 20

Jeb's arrest had hit his friends badly. They were shunned at school by the rest of their classmates.

"You hung with dat thug life," spat one of the older boys from the estate, cycling past them menacingly.

"We don't do murder of innocents round here. This is *our* ends. *We* got standards. *We* got honour."

"Watch your backs, you fucking scumbags! We're scoping you!" cried the bullies at school, in anger.

Finn, Tiny and Marcus were ostracised. There was no getting away from it. They were hated by association. They weren't spoken to at school by their peers, they weren't invited to parties on the estate, people's backs were turned every time they appeared.

They were afraid to walk out alone at certain times of the day.

"We're gonna get ya" was sprayed in large letters opposite Finn's flat.

Together the boys tried to make sense of it all, at their favourite spot, down near the canal. They had been seeing less of each other, trying to lie low socially. They walked together to school and from school and stayed together at break times, away from anyone else, afraid that they'd get shanked if they were ever alone.

"No fucking way!" Marcus kept repeating.

"Shit" said Finn, scratching his head. "I mean, what the fuck?" He couldn't make sense of it.

"Did he say anyfink to you?" they looked at Tiny.

Tiny shook his head silently, trying to digest the information that one of his closest friends had been arrested for the attempted rape and murder of some girl.

"He can't have done it," continued Marcus, "She was older than him. Was he dat strong?"

"Dunno," replied Tiny flatly. "He had been going to the gym lately to build himself up to maximum fitness, innit".

"Yeah, but that was to make the Midnight Basketball Team, bro, not for dis kind of shit".

"Why's everyone angry wiv us? We ain't done nufink. It's like people fink we was in on it and we wasn't," reasoned Finn.

"We got totally rinsed by that fucker! What an absolute dog!" shouted Tiny.

"Totally rinsed," spat Marcus in disbelief.

There followed a silence that seemed to last forever, but was only about 5 minutes long.

Marcus and Finn were gazing into the canal. The water was calm but their mood was edgy.

"I'm gonna split now," said Tiny, "laters, my mains" he said as he walked off.

"Yeah, safe" said Marcus. He had been focusing more and more on his studies, determined to get that apprenticeship which would take him from life on the Holmville and give him the chance at a career and the hope for the future that that would bring. He was lying low socially, hoping that he would eventually stop being tainted by association with Jeb.

"Laters," said Finn, but they all knew that their friendships were torn apart by Jeb's apparent random act of evil. Could they ever re-group again? Even if he was found innocent and released, they all felt as though these events had matured them to the point where they were questioning the value of still remaining in touch with each other. Guilt by association made them feel slightly ill at ease, even in each other's company. Even though they knew that, if Jeb had told them in advance of his plans, they wouldn't have been able to stop him. One thing about Jeb, he was very goal-orientated and determined.

Finn was fingering a spliff that he'd rolled and was in his pocket. He'd smoke it on his own. He felt alone and sad. Why had Jeb been such a stupid fucker and ruined it for all of them? What the hell had he been thinking?

"Loser!" shouted a younger youth, walking past Finn. Finn glowered at him and the youth ran off.

Tiny headed off into the Holmville Estate, glanced behind him, to check that no-one was looking, then took the stairwell to the second floor. On the second floor, he walked down the walkway, checking that he wasn't being followed, and stopped before a grey door. He knocked 4 times.

The door opened and he entered and walked through into the brightly-decorated living room.

Seated on cushions on the floor were Ahmed, Abdul Mutal, Zohair and Imam Ibrahim Nadir, known locally as Imam Ibrahim. Ahmed's younger brother, Sohail who had opened the door went into the kitchen and closed the door behind him. A strong smell of spices and cooked food wafted through the air from the kitchen. Tiny felt a pang of hunger. He hadn't eaten since lunchtime.

"Assalum aleikum, bruver," said Ahmed, looking up at Tiny.

"Please be seated," said Abdul Mutal, pointing to some cushions on the floor.

Imam Ibrahim was about 50 years of age. He had a long white beard and a wrinkled face. He wore traditional Pakistani clothing. He smiled kindly at Tiny.

"So, you want to become a Muslim?" he asked.

"Yes," replied Tiny.

Imam Ibrahim smiled and continued, "You have been learning the 5 Pillars of Islam?"

"Yes," replied Tiny, gesturing across the room, "with my brother, Zohair," and he looked across at Zohair who nodded approvingly.

"Tiny knows the Qur'an quite well already. He reads it in English every day and has started coming to evening prayers with us."

"And what Muslim name will you be taking?" asked the imam.

"Yusuf. I thought Yusuf was a nang sounding name," smiled Tiny. He then noticed their solemn faces, so he continued, "the lesson of the story of Yusuf is to forgive and forget the past." Tiny, looked at the floor and thought for a moment about his recent past and felt a pang of shame.

"A good choice of name," smiled the imam. They all smiled.

"So, Yusuf, you believe in Allah and his Prophet Muhammed, peace be upon him, sent by Allah to be a help to mankind?"

"I do, with all my heart," replied Tiny and he truly felt as if he believed it.

"So now we will say the Shahada, the Islamic declaration of faith, so that you can become a Muslim. First, repeat after me in English, 'There is no God but Allah, and Muhammad is his messenger.'"

Tiny repeated the words.

"Now we will say it in Arabic. Please repeat after me 'Ashhadu Alla Ilaha Illa Allah, Wa Ashhadu Anna Muhammad Rasulu Allah.' "

Tiny cleared his throat and repeated the words slowly.

"Allah Hamidallah!" cried Abdul Mutal, raising his eyes to the heavens.

"Allah HuAkbar!" exclaimed Zohair.

They all stood up and hugged Tiny.

Ahmed was beaming from ear to ear with genuine joy. "Welcome, brother," he said, when it was his turn to hug Tiny.

"You are a Muslim now, Yusuf" proclaimed the Imam joyfully, "Allah has forgiven all your past sins."

Tiny sighed deeply. It was exactly what he wanted to hear. He finally felt calm and at peace.

"I look forward to seeing you in the mosque," said Imam Ibrahim.

Tiny nodded, "Definitely."

Sohail brought in platters of hot food; pakoras, stuffed parathas with pickles and green tea with cardamom. They ate and drank, and discussed the Qur'an for several hours.

Tiny felt a part of something good. He felt accepted. For him, his life had new meaning now. He had distanced himself from those others. So-called friends. They weren't friends. They were just drug-taking alcoholics who sullied themselves with loose women. No, his Islamic brothers were now his friends. He had never felt such acceptance and love before. He was reluctant to leave this warm environment and return to his own home.

Meanwhile, elsewhere on the Holmville, Lucinda, Casey, Ashlee, Shamis and Shireen stood in the doorway of one of the entrances to the Holmville, shaking and silent. Shireen was crying. Big Earl's sister had gathered some of the older girls together, after school, and they had set upon them, pulling their hair, slapping and punching them. Casey had burn marks in her upper arm from the cigarette butts that were seared into her skin. The skin was scorched and it was painful. She was sobbing.

"Yo! My girls!" Shamis greeted them. They were all tearful.

"I got slapped and they said I was a sket because I'd got with Jeb," cried Casey.

"Did *you* get with Jeb?" asked Ashlee, angrily.

"No way?" asked Shamis, in shock.

"No, no," said Casey, who was in denial, and also afraid, "you just beggin' now. No way."

"Ashlee, what you sayin' is you're proud he was your man?" asked Lucinda.

"He was *never* my man!" snapped Ashlee, "Big Earl was my guy. Jeb was just there but he was no way my man, got it?!" she emphasised, angrily.

The girls nodded. There was no way they'd cross Ashlee. Inwardly Ashlee felt sick at the thought that she'd been with a potential rapist and murderer. The case had thrown up terrible things about Jeb. He loved violent pornography. He had no respect for women. He showed no remorse for his crime. Ashlee felt relieved that she'd had an abortion as soon as she'd found out that Jeb had made her pregnant. She wanted to offload that secret to her girls but she knew that she'd have to keep it forever.

"They said I was a loser for hanging with you," wept Shireen.

"They said I was a no-good junkie," spat Lucinda.

After 5 minutes of raised voices and sobbing, Casey finally spoke.

"Listen, my girls, just chillax, deep breath and chillax," said Casey, taking charge.

"We all know that Jeb was an evil, shit, fucking piece of low life scum. We didn't know nufink about him being mental and criminal, like. It's not our fault, right? He totally rinsed us, even his bros. They knew nutin'."

"Yeah, but people think we were a part of it," moaned Shireen.

Casey was rubbing her upper arm. The burn marks stung her flesh causing it to ache. She worried that she might be scarred for life. An eternal reminder of the boy she'd once slept with. She shuddered as she recollected the time that she'd slept with Jeb, behind the dustbins on the estate, and how rough he had been with her. She could've been raped. He had the strength and the inclination, apparently. She felt relieved that she'd got out of that one alive and that she was on the Pill, so there was no chance of getting pregnant from him. He hadn't wanted to wear a condom. The guy was clearly a maniac. She felt violated, even though it had been consensual. It would take her a long time to get over the experience. She felt so low about it that she wanted to cry.

"Think, what's gonna happen next? Every time we set foot outside our yard are we gonna get shanked? That ain't good, but I think now that it's happened, maybe we're gonna be ok."

"Jeb totally rinsed us out but this bad ting can bring us together," reasoned Ashlee, while pacing up and down.

"Group hug" said Lucinda, as they all gathered round and embraced each other.

"What do we do next?" asked Shireen, "I feel like getting fucked."

"How can you get fucked when we don't got no bevvies and no stuff?!" retorted Shamis.

"I got some spliff and some E's" smiled Lucinda.

"I think we need 'em," laughed Shamis, "but we can't go to the usual place to take 'em. They are probably scoping for us."

"My crib?" offered Casey.

"Yeah" was the group reply and they set off for Casey's 12th floor flat, with a feeling of safety in numbers, and a desire to melt their troubles and sorrows into drug-infused oblivion.

CHAPTER 21

The sun was shining, the air was crisp and there wasn't a cloud in the sky. It was the first day of the trial and Jeb Dunsmore was travelling to the courthouse cells by armoured van. He was handcuffed to a guard and sat opposite another guard. Jeb decided to look into the guard's eyes and try to psyche him out. The guard met Jeb's stare with a cold, disinterested one. He was used to these small time criminals trying to psyche him out. It was a game. He found that if he stared, coldly and blankly back at them for long enough, they soon gave up and tried to find some other way to amuse their psycho brains on the journey to the court.

Upon arrival at the court, Jeb was brought to the cells and met with Simeon. He changed into the suit that his mum had sent to him at the young offender's institute.

"Dunno why I couldn't have just got dressed there," he complained.

"Procedure," replied Simeon as he sat across the table from Jeb marking up some notes. He didn't look up at Jeb but felt Jeb's cold stare upon him, making him feel uneasy.

The cell door was unlocked and Emma McAdams joined them.

"Are you ok?" she asked Jeb.

"Got any gum?" was his reply.

Simeon looked up at that point and exchanged glances with Emma, who rummaged in her pocket and produced a piece of chewing gum. She handed it to Jeb. Simeon went back to his notes.

"Do I look fly in this suit?" chewed Jeb.

"You look fine," replied Emma. Simeon was absorbed in his paperwork.

"Remember," said Simeon, "Speak clearly, loudly and slowly. Look at the jury. Answer the questions, keep to the point."

"I'm buzzing," smiled Jeb. He felt unusually happy.

Emma McAdams sighed. "It's good that you feel confident, but you don't want to appear cocky." She was angry inside that this vile, young thug, who had taken the life of a young woman with such ease, was apparently so remorseless. She disliked Jeb with an intensity but inhaled deeply to keep herself calm and her mind focussed on her job. As a professional, she had to do the best for her client, but she was still uncomfortable in his presence.

Jeb arrogantly blew a large bubble and smirked at her.

Simeon got angry, "Listen, do you want to go to prison for life? This is not a joke. It's your future, so stop mucking about and start taking this seriously."

Jeb scowled. He didn't like this guy.

"What happens now?" he asked, drumming his fingers rhythmically on the table.

"We wait til we're called and then you go up into the dock."

"Safe" said Jeb. "I've seen this in movies, loadsa times and it was in dat rap video that I liked about that girl..." Jeb tailed off when he saw the puzzled looks on Simeon and Emma's faces. He realised that these were old people. Rich people. People who would never understand about being young and about his life. His mood was darkening. How could they help him? Then the image of Maya's lifeless body swam before his eyes. It sometimes did. He closed his eyes. He put a hand over his eyes. The image would not go away. He felt tears well up. He didn't want these two arseholes to see him crying, especially as they were his only chance at going free.

He swallowed hard, but then asked, "Can I see my mum, before I go in, like?"

"No," replied Simeon. "The trial is about to start."

"When you give evidence, do you want to swear on the bible?" asked Emma, hoping that by changing the subject it might lighten the atmosphere.

Jeb frowned. "I ain't religious."

"I gathered that," interjected Simeon, looking up at Jeb, "you'll either swear on a holy book, like the bible, or the Qur'an, or the Torah, if you're Jewish," he added, although he suspected that Jeb was a non-practicing Protestant.

Jeb angrily shook his head, "I ain't a yid!" he snarled, and clenched his fists.

Emma McAdams face darkened. She was finding it hard to maintain her composure before this odious youth. She squirmed in her seat. She had recently been dating a Jewish man and was falling quite deeply for him. She found Jeb's comments profoundly offensive.

Jeb sensed Emma's discomfort and said, "Oh, are you a yid then?"

Emma was taken aback. Simeon looked at her, interested in hearing her response.

"No, but my partner is!" she replied, as calmly as she could muster under the circumstances.

Jeb smirked, "they don't got no skins on their knobs, ha, but you probably know that anyway!" Jeb roared with laughter and rhythmically waved the clenched fist of his right hand in the air.

"Enough!" said Simeon, raising his voice, "I must insist you treat Ms McAdams with respect. You should apologise for that remark. It's not too late for either of us to decline to act for you. Think carefully." Simeon realised that he deeply despised this youth. It would be very hard to act in his best interests in court, knowing how horrid he really was. He felt as though the case was already lost. He therefore decided he would treat it as good practice for a future, better case. He would, obviously, act in his client's best interests but he knew that this would be an uphill struggle. How could they convince a jury that this knucklehead was innocent of the heinous crimes of which he stands accused? The guy could barely rustle up a brain cell. Maybe, Simeon thought, that would be the answer. The best way to put his case for the defence across would be to portray his client as a total idiot, incapable of harming anyone.

Emma McAdams had stood up and was facing the wall. She was furious with Jeb and furious with herself for being furious about Jeb's remarks. He was just some silly youth who would probably get put away for life. She shouldn't allow him the chance to have power over her. The last time he'd exerted power over a woman, he'd killed her.

"Sorrrrry," said Jeb in semi-mocking tones, and kicked out at the empty chair opposite him.

Simeon glared at him.

"No, I am soz, really, bare soz," said Jeb.

Emma admired Simeon's gallantry. She had felt like quitting the case. Then she reasoned that that would be deemed unprofessional, and even though she felt outraged, she sat down again at the table, regained a measure of her composure and continued, "or you'll make an affirmation. I can tell you that juries tend to like people who swear on a holy book, like the bible. It may sound old-fashioned but it gives more credence, er, more believability to their evidence. You'll be more convincing. So, if you're not offended by it, I'd advise you to swear on the bible."

"Ok," said Jeb, giving a thumbs-up sign, much to Simeon and Emma's surprise and relief.

"Safe. Makes sense," he continued and his mood started to lift again and the cell was filled with the noisy sound of chewing gum and chewing gum bubbles being blown and popped, which grated on Simeon and Emma's nerves. Jeb was silently thrilled that he was annoying them. He smirked while looking down at the table.

On her way to court, Harriet Wokingham, had performed her usual pre-trial rituals. She wheeled her wheel along case to the boot of her car and placed it inside, from the left hand side of the car. She wore a pair of shoes that she always wore when she won a case. "My victory shoes!" she chuckled to herself. She sat in the driver's seat and pressed the CD button on her in-car entertainment system. Vivaldi's *Four Seasons* auto selected and began to play on the eight-speaker stereo system. She loved it. It fired her up and put her in the right frame of mind for a day of legal wrangling. Harriet couldn't wait to see the jury. She was confident that she would soon have them onside. There *would* be justice for Maya Fullbright and closure for her poor parents. The sat-nav was programmed for Wood Green Crown Court in Haringey, north London. Harriet put the car into gear and set off from her driveway. She felt calm and confident and was inwardly smiling to herself.

"Turn left, third exit" said the standardised female sat-nav voice. Harriet smiled, the music of Vivaldi was elevating her spirit to a higher plane emotionally and she was definitely fired up and ready to do battle with the Defence in court.

Magda Jelovic had passed through the security checks and was now waiting in the jury area of Wood Green Crown Court. She had placed her belongings in a locker and sat down to read her book. Three other groups had been counted out to make up a jury, but it was now 10:45am and she hadn't yet been called. Perhaps she wouldn't be called at all. She sighed, bored and ate an apple. She had been there since 9:00am, like most of the other jurors.

An older woman with curly blonde hair and a pock-marked face leaned forward towards her. "I've done jury service before. You could wait ages until you get called," the friendly lady added. Magda eyed her intently. "Sometimes, you're not called at all!" laughed the lady. She munched on a chocolate bar.

"I tell ya, it was a drugs case," continued the woman, "and I was foreman of the jury," she added proudly. "I told the other jurors that he looked guilty and so we should convict him. Well, it was getting late and we wanted to get home for our tea."

"But that's not allowed, no?" said Magda in shock. "I thought a jury has to listen to the evidence." Magda had a strong sense of justice and knew that she wanted to do things properly.

"Well, they're supposed to," laughed the woman, "but you can always tell when they look guilty, and believe me, he looked guilty" she continued conspiratorially, then upon realising that Magda looked unimpressed, she continued, "I suppose it's different in your country."

Magda was thinking up a suitable reply when a court clerk appeared and started reciting names from a list. "Magda Jelovic" was mentioned. Magda almost clapped. Magda was to be a juror in the case of *R. v Jebson Dunsmore*. She wondered what it was all about. She hadn't been following the news of Maya Fullbright's murder. She was aware of a murder being headline news but she didn't really take it in at the time.

"Follow me," said the court clerk, leading the jury to the lifts. There was a buzz of muted chatter surrounding the jury.

"I think it might be that murder case that was big on the news last year. You know, the one with that poor girl who worked at the coffee shop." one of them exclaimed.

"Oh yes, the pretty lass that was strangled to death" replied another juror, "could this be that case? I think he was called Jeb something or other, wasn't he?"

The court clerk took them all up to the jury room and explained, briefly, court procedure, before distributing notepads and pens, and collecting everyone's mobile phone from them. Finally, she led them into the courtroom, where they were sworn in.

Magda took her seat and spotted a thin woman in barrister's robes wearing a wig, peering over some notes. Further along, a very tall, thin man in barrister's robes stood wearing a wig. He was whispering to a woman who was standing behind him.

Magda glanced around the public gallery. People were starting to fill it. She noticed a woman that she had seen a lot in the newspapers, seated next to a man, who appeared to be holding her hand. The lady looked very sad. Some young people were seated a few rows behind her, one in Islamic dress. Magda soaked up the atmosphere. She didn't notice as Tom Rolandson slipped into the public gallery and sat down quietly at the back. He sighed deeply.

"All rise" said the court clerk as the judge entered the room.

"Bring in the defendant."

Jeb, handcuffed to a security guard was brought up from the cells in a lift. He was led from the lift to the defendant's entrance to the courtroom. Before he entered the dock, he took a deep breath. He felt sweat dripping down his back, saturating the lower part of his shirt.

"Ok?" asked the guard who was handcuffed to Jeb. He was used to prisoners being nervous. Jeb nodded. Another guard unlocked the door to the defendants' entrance to the courtroom. There were some steps to ascend. Jeb walked through the door and tried to go up the steps but his legs suddenly felt heavy as lead. He had to force them to move. They wouldn't move. He was suddenly absolutely terrified. Rooted to the spot. What would he do? He looked like a coward. He was angry with his body for letting him down at this crucial moment, just as it had when he had tried to rape that stupid Maya wotsits and ended up killing the screaming bitch instead. He swallowed hard and adjusted his tie.

Then he closed his eyes for a moment and imagined that he was Ati Adeofale stepping out with the team at the Champions League final. He imagined that the Champions League theme tune was playing and that the court would be like a football pitch. He'd be the star. There was nothing to fear.

Without a backward glance, Jeb raised his head and stepped forward into the dock. All eyes were upon him.

EPILOGUE

Six months later.

"In the name of the Father, and of the Son and of the Holy Spirit. Amen."

On a breezy picturesque hilltop in Newcastle, County Wicklow, Ireland, Father Monaghan made the sign of the cross and stepped back from the graveside. The weather was dry and sunny and the sound of sobbing could be heard as Molly Molson's coffin was lowered into the grave. Her daughters, Brenda and Teresa gripped each other's arms tightly for support. Tears streamed down their faces as they threw some earth onto the coffin and mumbled, "Goodbye Mum." They turned round and set off, walking arm in arm, towards Flannery's pub, which was a five minute walk from the cemetery and where their mother's wake would be held. Their husbands and children walked behind them.

The whole village had gathered at the picturesque, hillside church. Amongst the assembled crowd, one face stood out. It was that of Runi Lancel.

Inside the quaint and cosy pub, they sat with whiskies while plates of sandwiches were passed around. The place was heaving with people. "It was a good send off," said Brenda to her husband Seamus, who nodded. "Mum woulda loved it," said Teresa. At that moment Runi approached them with a pint of Guinness in his hand. "Hello," he said warmly, "I used to live in the same block of flats as your mother, Mrs Molson, when she lived in London. I found out she'd passed away and I wanted to come here to pay my respects."

Brenda and Teresa looked up at him, as he continued, "She was a lovely lady, your mum. I was very fond of her."

"Are you Runi Lancel?" asked Brenda.

Runi was surprised. "Yes. Yes, I am."

"Our mother" chimed Brenda, "said you were a grand fella. Always helping her with things. Weren't you working with them feckin' bastard youths?"

Runi nodded and smiled slightly.

"And you came all the way over from London?"

"Uhm. Er, yes, I was, but I live in Ireland now. Dublin, in fact. I'm a youth worker there," he elaborated, smiling and taking a sip of his Guinness.

Runi didn't tell them that during Jeb's trial, his Midnight Basketball scheme had collapsed. The police investigation into the murder had put an unwanted spotlight on the Holmville Estate again. There was infighting amongst the youths as the community was split apart, and they weren't turning up to training sessions, so funding was withdrawn. In addition he'd been tense and on edge since learning that Raydon Darnell had been killed by the police in a drugs raid. Runi knew that as long as Raydon was alive, no-one would bother him, but with Raydon's death there would be turf wars.

He had fled to Ireland. First to Belfast and then down to Dublin, where he had found employment as a youth worker in a rundown part of town.

"What happened to that scum lad, who killed that poor, wee lass?" continued Teresa, "such a shocking business. Poor mum was very upset by it all. Her health deteriorated shortly after she got here but I'm so glad we got her out of there."

"Jeb? He got 15 years. 12 for murder and 3 for attempted rape," replied Runi, "he'll do the first part of his sentence in the young offenders institute, then when he's 20 he'll be moved to prison."

Runi's thoughts turned to Jeb's future wasted years in prison. He hoped that at least when released, the boy would embrace his second chance and turn his life around. Runi knew more than most what it meant to make the right decisions in life.

June Dunsmore had given up her flat on the Holmville Estate and was now living with her boyfriend, Rob Dansley, in his small, rented flat in Finsbury Park. Apart from a smell of damp and some mould on the bathroom ceiling, June was happy with the move. They both still worked at the bus depot but had managed to re-arrange their shifts so that they could spend as much time with each other as possible.

June never received visitation papers to visit Jeb. He never wrote to her or came to the phone when, at the beginning of his incarceration, she'd tried to call. She realised, somewhat sadly, that he didn't want to keep up a relationship with her. It was very hard to accept on many levels. June couldn't feel comfortable when she thought about Jeb and his terrible crime. It made her mentally restless. She learnt how to put him out of her mind. Yet when her work colleagues talked about what their children were up to, June felt a pang in her heart and her expression would sadden. Jeb was her only child. She wouldn't ever consider having anymore. If Rob was there, he would pick up on her mood and change the subject, which made everyone feel uncomfortable, as they then remembered Jeb and felt pity for June.

There was nothing June could do about Jeb and no point beating herself up anymore. Her life was with Rob now. He made her laugh, he doted on her. She was in love with him. Sometimes she would wake up and wonder how different her life could have been, but being a realist and a survivor, she knew that she would make the best of whatever life threw at her.

The pouring rain bouncing off the windows of the young offenders institute was driving Jeb mad. He was sitting in the dining room playing with the slop they called food. He hated the young offender's institute. He hated his mother. He hated his life. He hated his so-called friends who never visited him. He hated the other youths here. He hated the imam that visited them, and the vicar, who tried to be so cool but was actually a prat because of it. He hated everything and everyone. The only good thing was that a man, who claimed to be his father, had started visiting him. Jeb could sense he was a weak man and a soft touch, so he'd played on the man's guilt and the man had been giving him money.

Jeb's heart had hardened. He would show them all. He would bide his time and channel his growing anger. He couldn't wait till the day of his release, when he knew he would show them who was boss.

On a different day, it would all be exactly the same.

Printed in Great Britain
by Amazon

40461095R00162